The Black Dreams:
Strange Stories from
Northern Ireland

The Black Dreams:
Strange Stories from Northern Ireland

Edited by
Reggie Chamberlain-King

·THE·
BLACK
·STAFF·
PRESS

First published in 2021 by Blackstaff Press
an imprint of Colourpoint Creative Ltd
Colourpoint House
Jubilee Business Park
21 Jubilee Road
Newtownards BT23 4YH

With the assistance of the Arts Council of Northern Ireland

Printed and bound by CPI Group UK Ltd, Croydon CR0 4YY

A CIP catalogue record for this book is available from the British Library

ISBN 978 1 78073 328 9

www.blackstaffpress.com

For my beautiful friend LD (1964–2020).
We were working on ghost stories together.
Perhaps we still are.

'When I was five the black dreams came;
Nothing after was quite the same.'

Louis MacNeice, *from* 'Autobiography'

Contents

Introduction

Dreaming the Black Dream

'When I say that Belfast is dominated by a dream, I mean it
in the strict psychological sense; that something inside
the mind is stronger than everything outside it. Nonsense is
not only stronger than sense, but stronger than the senses.'
G.K. Chesterton, *Irish Impressions*, 1919

I don't recall if I saw my first gunman in my childhood nightmares or on my childhood streets. There were plenty in both and they looked very much like each other. The things my mother warned would happen to little boys who spoke to soldiers or travelled by taxi soon happened to other people – it was frequently in the news. She was anxious about many things, and stories were her way of sharing them with me. Her warnings were partway between fairy tale and premonition, a magical act of manifestation. It became easy to believe, then, all the other stories. For example, there were devil worshippers sacrificing dogs on Black Mountain. And when it was suggested that those stories were actually planted by the military as part of British psy-ops, that was easy to believe as well. Everything was possible. I borrowed *The Prophecies of Nostradamus* many times from the Falls Library and was able to match each news headline with one of its vague quatrains. Fear is a function of imagination and one lives in it as fully as a dream – the same laws apply. There is something inside the mind stronger than everything outside it and physics only asserts itself on the occasions when the dream meets the reality, when bomb scare becomes bomb.

When G.K. Chesterton visited Ireland in 1919, he was surprised by the 'sleepless' Irish: 'If a dream haunts them, it is rather as something that escapes them; and indeed some of their finest poetry is rather about seeking fairyland than about finding it.' However, there was one place in Ireland where he seemed to find 'the dream itself in possession; as one might see from afar a cloud resting on a single hill. There, a dream, at once a desire and a delusion, brooded above a whole city. That place was Belfast.'

And not just Belfast, I would say. A dream possesses all of Northern Ireland and Northern Ireland is a sort of fairyland too. It is a place of outspoken symbols and unspoken rules, where only local logic applies. Strangers finding themselves lost there may find themselves lost there. And the dreamers who inhabit the place are safe as long as they don't wake up. They sleepwalk, sleepwork, sleepwatch, and sleepwait, living inside the mind, eyes wide shut to what is outside it.

Dreamers march along their dream streets and we get out of the way, as though their streets had as much claim to the space as ours. Walking among them, we must be conscious of their dreams and the shapes they take. There is nostalgia, for one, and there is idealism: a dreamed-of past and a dreamed-of future. There is anxiety, fear, and denial as well. It is easier to live in those fairylands than in the reality. However, the insistence of the dreamers makes their dream a reality for us too, blurring the line between the sleeping and the waking world.

And so you find yourself in a dream as well, ever ready for someone else's dream to intrude. Even in the quiet moments, one is alert to sudden change, to a rude awakening. You are set to go from resting to racing on a hair trigger. You are full of this energy and it has to go somewhere.

I put it into monster movies, ghost stories, and fantasies – a safe place to be afraid, because, in a ghost story, *something* must happen. Then, when the something happens, it's over and you are still in the library or on the sofa with the curtains drawn. The whole time, your imagination is under the bridle of a benevolent author: Poe, M.R. James, Kafka, Machen, Shelley; dream dwellers like me, funnelling their own troubled states into stories.

The landscape of their tales was a familiar one. A feeling of unease permeates the text. An expectation. But the expected thing is absent or an unexpected thing is present. There are forces you choose not to see, or can't see, but they are perpetually in motion. There is secret knowledge, a hidden order of men or monsters at work beneath the surface: they are under the rules of fairyland; they are as real as dreams and, as such, more like life to me than the Kevin and Sadie books we read in school. They mapped out the emotional, if not the actual, geography of growing up and living here.

I am not entirely sure what to call this type of story that so fully captured my experience and imagination. Ghost story seems inadequate, as there is so rarely a ghost, even when the story purports to be from real life. When I was young, there was, reputedly, a poltergeist resident in a house in Beechmount, but one refrained from remarking on it just as you would have if a schoolmate was being raised by their grandparents or a supposed uncle.

Fairy tale is inappropriate, as it has now come to suggest a morality tale, when the fairyland I know is completely amoral. Roald Dahl wrote *Tales of the Unexpected*, which spoils the surprise I always thought, while the 'weird' of *Weird Tales* magazine and weird fiction is an awfully weighty adjective. These stories are light, like a mist – they cloud your vision.

The old, psychedelic annual that my mother locked in the wardrobe to curb the worst of its effects was called *Tales to Tremble By*. The wardrobe was obviously ineffective; the green-skinned woman who cackled against the red-purple vortex of the book's cover was already in my head. And stayed there, long after I went to sleep. She was always there.

Really, these are dream stories. That's what I want to call them. Dream stories, such as the dreamers tell themselves as they march the streets of their imagination. And the dream mode has always sounded in art from the northern part of Ireland, as early as the visions of St Colum Cille. The dream is present as the harbinger clowns and moons in the paintings of Gerard Dillon. The dream is there is in the plays of Stewart Parker, whether as the reminiscing ghosts of *Pentecost* and *The Iceberg* or the reveries of *I'm A Dreamer, Montreal*. It is there in Brian Moore. It is an escape in Owen McCafferty's *Mojo Mickybo*. The young fellas of the title slide between this world and the cowboy films they love. Those fantasies of the western allow them to be heroes who can survive the Troubles. I suppose I did the same with horror films, although there are no heroes in the stories I liked.

Whether wittingly or not, Northern Ireland's great pop tradition resides in the dreamscape of nostalgia, both potent and paralysing. What is 'Cyprus Avenue' but a dream of the past, a dream of a love that isn't or never was? Nostalgia holds back Feargal Sharkey – or whoever replaced him in The Undertones – when he cannot beat teenage dreams. Even at eighteen, Tim Wheeler of Ash was looking backward, wishing to reside in the perfect summer of 'Oh Yeah'. All looking back to a time before the trouble started. Only Stiff Little Fingers look forward to an 'Alternative Ulster'.

The novelist Forrest Reid, Northern Ireland's most dedicated dreamer, set his work in the space between childhood and adulthood. Having attempted suicide as a teen, afraid to grow up, afraid of his adult sexuality, he knew the allure of nostalgia and paid the price for romanticism. His stories occupy a place between the two. There are multiple dreams and Reid's dream stories represent the ones I most easily understand: full of wonder and anxiety and uncertainty. To differentiate them from the metaphysics of C.S. Lewis or 'pataphysics of Flann O'Brien, I will borrow Robert Aickman's term: they are 'strange stories'; stories of in-between states, of unstable realities, of the unreliability of our understanding. It is no surprise that, like the people in Beechmount, the young Reid lived with a ghost on Mount Charles in Belfast. His story 'Courage' is one of the most widely-anthologised ghost stories ever written.

There have been other writers of strange stories from the north of Ireland. Forrest Reid's young disciple, Stephen Gilbert, wrote several remarkable Ulster novels that develop and twist the traits associated with his teacher, charting a troubled relationship between the two men. In *Monkeyface*, a chimpanzee is brought to Belfast, where he is taught to speak and be an upstanding Ulsterman, but he dreams of running back to the jungle. In *The Burnaby Experiments*, a young man with no prospects is forced to share his body with his ageing, eccentric mentor. Gilbert's final novel, published in 1968, is perhaps the most successful piece of strange fiction from Northern Ireland. *Ratman's Notebooks*, an international bestseller, sees the bullied son of a dead businessman befriend a nest of rats in his garden. The maladjusted youth trains them into an army to overthrow his father's successor at what was the family firm. It is a peculiar revenge fantasy that became the cult movie *Willard* and started the film franchise that gave us Michael Jackson's paean to a pest, 'Ben'.

Around the same time, the acclaimed children's author Martin Waddell began his career writing for Herbert van Thal's popular *Pan Book of Horror Stories* anthologies, producing numerous stories under his own name and a variety of pseudonyms. Although Waddell would employ the supernatural and the strange in his award-winning children's books, these early stories are marked by their macabre wit and cruelty. Waddell stands apart as being the only Irish writer to have a story – 'Whisper' – adapted for Rod Serling's TV show, *Night Gallery*.

However, the seam of strangeness in Northern Irish literature predates these writers. History hasn't always remembered these predecessors fondly for their excursions into the weird, but, for some, it has been the saving of them. I have largely considered it my duty to seek such writers out. Mrs Charlotte Riddell of Carrickfergus was a popular, hard-working author of City of London novels. She is now better remembered for her collection *Weird Stories* and her much-anthologised Victorian ghost tales on Irish themes. Rosa Mulholland, born in High Street, Belfast, in 1841, is another successful author whose lengthy novels of rural Irish life have been largely forgotten, while her short, strange stories have found renewed life. A close friend of Charles Dickens, her weird tales, also frequently on Irish themes, appeared in his magazine *All the Year Round* alongside Wilkie Collins and J.S. Le Fanu. Frances Browne, 'the Blind Poet of Ulster', was best known for her collection of children's stories, *Granny's Wonderful Chair*, but published a wide variety of strange tales in the popular Victorian periodicals.

Not all such writers incorporated Irish themes into their writing, especially in the twentieth century. Frank Frankfort Moore, student at the Royal Belfast Academical Institution, pro-Union journalist, and brother-in-law to Bram Stoker, set his 1905 collection, *The Other World*, in Ireland, England, the Mediterranean, and the coast of Africa. Mayne Reid, son of Ballyroney, County Down, was a veteran of the American-Mexican War and set his many strange adventure stories along that southern frontier. *The Headless Horseman*, his best-remembered novel, was beloved by Teddy Roosevelt, Vladimir Nabokov, and Czesław Miłosz. Larne-born journalist, James M'Henry, set his Gothic novels in the forests of New England, where he immigrated in the nineteenth century, while Beatrice

Grimshaw, the explorer and travel journalist, published several collections of weird tales based on her experiences in the South Seas.

The peculiarities of Ulster are rarely presented in these stories, even those with an Irish theme. In Mary Shelley's *Frankenstein*, the monster and the man both find themselves shipwrecked on the 'detested shore' of Ireland's north coast, where the man is tried for the monster's crimes. The awkward geography of these scenes makes it clear that, for Shelley, Ulster was a concept of strangeness rather than an experienced reality. We might surmise that the 'county town' in which Victor Frankenstein faces justice is Ballyshannon in County Donegal, birthplace of Shelley's grandmother, Elizabeth Dixon. However, that detail is no more important than if it were Carrickfergus or Coleraine. It is all the same 'wretched country'.

Writers from the North may have been too close to represent the region's complexities, but they were not disassociated from its political and cultural turmoil. George W. Russell, the mystic and fantasist known as Æ, is now most closely associated with Dublin and Irish nationalism, but was born and raised in Lurgan, ever 'grateful to Providence for the mercy shown ... in removing [him] from Ulster.' The Belfast Quaker Herbert Moore Pim played his part in the Easter Rising, standing in a field in Coalisland that Easter morning, and contributing his speculative serial, 'The Supermaniac', to the republican magazine *The Irishman*. Although his strange novels take place in England, the conflicts and the idiosyncratic concerns of his homeland are evident in them: in *The Man with Thirty Lives*, a London dandy deals with the legacy of Catholic persecution with a time-travelling wizard; in *The Pessimist*, an Ulster philosopher must decide if he ends the world's suffering by ending the world. In a life as strange as any story, Pim changed his political allegiance in 1919, becoming a vocal unionist, and spent time in a French mental hospital.

In 1921, the Professor of Celtic Languages at Queen's University, Anglican minister F.W. O'Connell, began writing his collection of strange stories, *The Fatal Move*, under the pseudonym Conall Cearnach. Although, pointedly, none of the stories take place in what was then becoming Northern Ireland, that political upheaval is felt through the whole collection. In the title story, two bitter rivals, once best friends, play a fatal game of chess using a set of ancient Irish chessmen; one of them will die when they make the wrong move. In another story, sectarian conflict between the Muslims and Hindus of India leaves a legacy that haunts the combatants even after death. And, in the future imagined in 'The Rejuvenation of Ivan Smithovitch', where the language has been politicised out of existence, the last surviving speaker of Cockney English comes to the door of a Gaeilgeoir seeking sanctuary.

Whether consciously or unconsciously, the strange story gave O'Connell the vocabulary and techniques to convey the strangeness of the new state in which he was living. Dreams, when interpreted, tell us the emotional truth. So, there are ghosts in the plays of Stewart Parker, because the Troubles was haunted by and begets ghosts. If the weird intrudes on the post-conflict writing of Anna Burns or Jan Carson, that is because the weird was there at the time of writing. Some may call that work magic realism, but, for me, they are just strange stories. That is the vocabulary I learned.

The strangeness of the story does not have to reflect the strangeness of the place. There can be a connection with strangeness as an experience in itself. Nobody wants to hear you describe your dream, but everyone understands the feeling of a dream. The American writer W.H. Pugmire was a closeted gay Mormon who was sent on his mission in 1972. He brought the message of Joseph Smith – half-heartedly – to the people of Omagh, in the most volatile year of the Troubles. He said he spent his time dodging bullets and being bored – there were no cinemas where he could watch monster movies like he used to do at home. In a second-hand shop in the town, he found a collection containing H.P. Lovecraft's 'The Haunter of the Dark', which presented him with an entirely new reading experience. Before he went back to the States, he had written and published his first strange story.

I don't know that Wilum Hopfrog Pugmire was influenced by the Northern Irish landscape or the conflict in which he found himself: he had his own anxieties to deal with. But

I often think that someone in Omagh had read that book before him. And, if he didn't want to weigh himself down crossing the Atlantic, someone in Omagh may have read it after him. These people found a common experience and language in Lovecraft's tales of unspeakable, unidentifiable horror. It is the feeling, as difficult as it is to describe, that we all share in, not the story.

When I came to compile this collection of strange stories, it was my dream – at once a desire and a delusion – to capture my uneasy feeling of growing up in Northern Ireland, the same feeling that was safely contained in a bank holiday horror film or *Tales to Tremble By*: things are not as they seem. That the authors of these stories have managed to distil that uncertainty in many different ways, in many different parts of Northern Ireland, at different times, shows just how much that feeling permeates the imagination here. We all have our own anxieties.

My definition of Northern Irish was purposefully wide. Some of the authors grew up here; some did not. Some moved here and others moved away. They are not of any specific nationality or tradition. They come from no particular community but the community of dreamers. And, for this collection, they sought fairyland and found it.

Reggie Chamberlain-King
Whitehead
July 2021

The Black

Ian Sansom

MY brother said that he needed to dampen down the colours in his flat. There was too much colour in there. There was too much confusion. The colours were clashing. They were humming, the colours. There was too much going on. That's what he said: there was too much going on.

First he did the walls, and then he did the skirting boards, and the ceiling. And then the doors. Carefully, methodically, over the course of a couple of weeks, he stripped them, primed them and painted them. He did a good job. He painted them all – carefully, methodically. He painted them black.

We explained to him that under the terms of his tenancy agreement he was not allowed to paint the walls, or the doors, or the ceilings. He was not allowed to redecorate. He wasn't allowed to make any alterations to the flat. He certainly wasn't allowed to paint it black.

Then he painted the furniture. I have to admit, it was quite skilfully done. He did the chairs first. And then the table. He used a kind of high gloss paint for the furniture. I don't know where he got it from. I suppose the local DIY place. It's difficult to say what they looked like, the table and chairs. They looked quite good. Sort of Scottish. Irish. Scandi. European. Something. The next time we came to visit he had moved on to the wardrobe and his bed – anything made of wood, or MDF. The kitchen units. Bathroom cabinet. I thought it was odd. But I thought that was it.

The next time we visited he'd done the sofa. It was sticky. Unusable. And in the kitchen he'd painted the fridge black, inside and out. There was a black bottle of milk, black cups and saucers. He'd painted the bathroom: the tiles, the floor, the mirror, the bath. The carpets.

'Can you not hear it?' he said. He could still hear it. He could still see it.

'Hear what?' I said.

We had him sectioned. It was some kind of episode, said the GP. He was sectioned for his own safety.

We visited him in the hospital, which was a dreadful place, much worse than I expected. I didn't think places like that existed any more.

He was allowed to wear an eye mask, so he didn't have to see all the colours. They'd administered high doses of sedatives, but even with the drugs he complained about the colours.

He had always been outgoing and gregarious, my brother. He was a real life-and-soul-of-the-party type. He could play the piano – self-taught – and he had a nice voice. He would often burst into song. He'd done well at school. Top of the class. In his teens he'd got a place at university but had dropped out after a year. He went travelling to South America. On his return he was a bit subdued, less likely to burst into song. But he got a job in what was then the local DHSS office, a clerical job, and he seemed happy enough. We never thought he'd marry but in his late twenties he met this woman through a dating agency. Whirlwind romance. They got married. But then they split up – within months they split up – for reasons that were never entirely clear.

He started to suffer from anxiety and depression. It became difficult to calm him down. He couldn't sleep. At night he started drinking heavily, in order to sleep.

His emotionality was high – that's what the GP said, when we went to see the GP. His emotionality. Your brother is emotionally labile, said the doctor. I didn't know what it meant. What I did know was that being emotionally labile left him exhausted all the time. Within half an hour of getting up he needed to go straight back to bed. He couldn't concentrate. His work suffered. They put some kind of performance management measures into place, and then he was dismissed. Which was when he started the painting.

They eventually found his body, deep in the woods. It was

painted completely black. The full details were never released – the police feared copycats.

All this was years ago now. Twenty years, almost. My parents are long dead. My brother. My children are all grown up and have left home.

For me, it started with my nails. I usually wore red. Then my hair.

I can feel it now.

Original Features

Jo Baker

I**T'S** really just a two-up-two-down, with an extra bit tacked on at the back to accommodate a narrow kitchen, and, above, a tiny bathroom and box room. It's not quite the dream home that many of Róisín's friends have somehow already achieved, but with Sean just starting his placement at the Royal, and Róisín on the first rung of the teaching payscale, it's all they can afford.

The kitchen, which will have to wait, is an assemblage of junk. A cracked Belfast sink, an unsteady electric cooker that burns her every time she looks at it, a leaking fridge, and an old House-Proud inhabited by silverfish. There's no garden, just an L-shaped concrete yard, with a meat safe nailed to the back wall, and glass shards set into the capstones, that catch the light at certain times of day and throw patches of green and brown around the narrow space. The back rooms don't get much light at all, and the bathroom is practically a cupboard, with a stained enamel bath taking up the entire length; it's so long that Róisín can lie flat on her back in it, as though in a coffin.

A fixer upper, in an up-and-coming area, the estate agent had said. Except that now they've bought it, there's no money left to fix it up.

But the sitting room is lovely, with an art deco fireplace and big bay window; it won't cost much to strip the floors. They'll squeeze bookshelves and a desk into the box room; it's no hardship for them to share a study. They have no curtains yet, but the bedroom window looks out into the stirring green of a lime tree, and once the new bed has been delivered, the futon can go in the second bedroom and there you have it: guest room. It's just around the corner from the Ormeau Bakery, so the smell of baking drifts deliciously down the street.

They pull up carpets and sand down floorboards. They strip paper in great tongues from off the walls. They have sex on the rug newly bought from Habitat. They climb into the old bath together and soak off the dust and grime and sweat.

'To think she brought up six kids here. The old lady. Six kids. How do you *do* that, how do you even fit them in, six kids, in a house like this?'

'Three sets of bunk beds,' he says, 'Boom.'

At night, the streetlamp projects a shadowplay of leaves across the bedroom. In the morning, bakery vans turn in the street, and the sun floods in. The light wakes her early, directly from a dream. She was carrying a tray teetering with fancy breakfast things – eggshell porcelain, glimmering cutlery – through from the dining room. But at the foot of the stairs there's a door that she had never noticed before.

The door is raw, freshly painted, rougher-hewn than the others, and slightly out of true. It's jammed awkwardly up against the bottom step. How can she not have noticed it before?

She turns the handle, pushes. The door opens into a quiet, spacious room with white walls and pale furniture. A skylight shows a patch of cool blue sky. Here and there are archways on to other spaces. French windows open on to green. They should spend time in there. It's beautiful. She's excited; she'll tell Sean.

In the bedroom, she goes to touch his shoulder, but when her hand reaches his skin, it's she who jolts awake, the bedroom a headache of livid morning light.

Her fingertips brush bare plaster as she descends the stairs. Beyond the wall is next door's sitting room with its blue Draylon sofa, where Martin and Andy prop up their guitars and heap videos and books, and hang their shirts to dry from their curtain rails, and scandalise Mrs Dawson on the other side with their casual ways. And that is all there is. But still, something of the dream lingers about the place.

'Lining paper,' Sean says later that same day, nodding to the hallway, the raw state of which he only now seems to notice. 'That'd cover it all up quare and handy.'

'Okay, good.'

It's just another job to add to an ever-expanding list; she doesn't expect anything to happen soon. But on Sean's next day off, his dad comes over, Volvo groaning with gear. Radio on, kettle on, swigging mug after mug of tea, pasting and smoothing and slicing with outsized scissors that make her feel like the dolls are decorating their own dolls' house, Sean and his dad paper the hallway, stairs, and landing, in flat matte paper, the colour of old teeth.

Sometimes she runs her fingertips over that patch of wall when she's passing by, but she doesn't mean anything by it. All that remains of the dream is the feeling: anticipatory, expansive.

The baby wails. She scrambles out of bed and staggers through to his room. She touches her hand to his forehead.

'Oh no, little guy.'

She strips him to his nappy, lifts him; his skin burns against her skin. He stops wailing for a moment, pushes away to stare at her and blink and rub his face with a fist. In their bedroom, Sean turns, mutters. He's back on earlies again tomorrow.

'I'm on it,' she says. 'Go you back to sleep.'

In the kitchen, little Nially sucks Calpol from the syringe and goes quiet. She carries him upstairs, but the moment she tries to put him down again, he wails. She hoicks him back up, bobs and sways and pats and sings, and none of this has any effect. She pads downstairs again and walks circuits round the ground floor: sitting room, hallway, dining room, kitchen; dining room, hallway, sitting room, dining room. The baby goes soft, finally; his head rests in the crook of her neck.

She sits down. The green velour chair they picked up in the Oxfam shop on the Dublin Road is upright but forgiving; she leans back and Niall lies against her, sweaty, snuffling. She'll wait until he's completely gone. She blinks, yawns quietly but so wide that it makes a creak. She blinks at the hallway, flooded with orange light from the streetlamp outside. She blinks slow blinks.

The door is now newer than it used to be. Whiter, more raw. It brings with it a sense of contained excitement: Christmas Eve, school holidays, but also an uneasy sense of obligation. It's just there, just a few steps away, opening on to all that beauty, all that space, and all she has to do is get up and walk three steps and open it. But she won't, she can't. She can't move an inch.

She blinks awake: the baby breathes against her chest, his shoulder blades softly moving under her hand. He heaves his head to one side, stuffs a thumb into his wet mouth, and sleeps on. And when she looks up the door is gone.

———

Little Orla is as pale as a beluga whale, her eyes an unsettling Wedgewood blue. She seems at first a placid creature; after her last feed of the day, she'll drop into a sleep so deep that you can change her nappy or her onesie and she doesn't even blink. But at two years old, some inner shift causes her to scream out in the night, making Róisín lurch awake, shreds of dream falling from her, scraps of white, her own hand reaching out for something just beyond her grasp.

In her box room cot, the girl lies, belly heaving, eyes wide, but asleep. They've been told they mustn't wake her, so Róisín soothes her till the shape of her sleep changes. Then Róisín shambles off to the sofa and wraps herself in a blanket and reads until the adrenalin fades out and leaves her limp. She might get a few hours' sleep too, after that.

The nights when the child doesn't cry out, Róisín sleeps dreamlessly. At least, she doesn't remember her dreams.

Róisín and Sean talk about therapies and techniques, but no sooner is a course of action decided upon than there'll be a spate of quiet nights, and they'll think the child is better, and let the matter slide. And when the night terrors come storming back, they can always find an explanation; teething, a bug, starting nursery, starting school; she will get over it, she will grow out of it. She just hasn't yet. When it's at its worst, Róisín drags out the old futon, and sleeps on the box room floor, so that when Orla starts to stir and whimper in the night, she can soothe her, and coax her back, without having to fully wake up herself.

One Saturday morning, bringing the kids back from the

park, Róisín falls into step with old Mrs Dawson outside the closed-down bakery. They walk along the street together, Orla's tiny cold hand in Róisín's, Niall racing on ahead on his scooter to stare at the oily goings-on at the garage.

'She has the night terrors,' Róisín explains, glancing down to catch Orla's unblinking gaze. 'I'm sorry if it's been disturbing you.'

'Poor wee scrap. What in under God have you been dreaming about, pet?'

Orla, china eyes fixed on Mrs Dawson, slowly shakes her head.

'The walls are so thin, I'm worried she'll wake the whole street.'

Mrs Dawson waves the concerns away. 'She'll grow out of it, you'll see.'

'We live in hope. But she only has to squeak now and I'm on edge. I don't know how she coped, the old lady who was there before us, bringing up six kids in that house. I mean how do you do that?'

'Ada?' A shrug. 'She just got on with it. It's what you did.'

The fluster of an autumn term pick-up, tired grubby damp kids, traffic, rain, squabbling. In the hall, Niall casually lobs his PE kit so that the bag slides along the tiles on its plastic studs and comes to a halt across the threshold of where the door would be, if the door were really there. Róisín feels a jolt of instinctive, sick unease.

'Take your stuff up to your room, please.'

'In a minute.'

Niall pushes through to the kitchen; she follows; he pours cordial into a glass, turns the tap.

'Just take your PE kit upstairs. I'm not expecting you to wash it or put it away or anything ridiculous like that. Just take it up.'

'Jeesh. In a *minute*.'

Scuffling on the stairs. When she goes back through, Orla, tiny elf-child Orla, eleven years old and looking more like eight, is hauling Niall's kitbag up the steps.

'Don't you do that for him,' Róisín says. 'He can do that himself.'

Orla simply says, 'It was in the way.'

Orla moves the pasta round in her bowl.

'Eat your dinner, sweetheart.'

The girl glances up at her mother, eyes huge under minky eyebrows.

'Don't you like it? I thought you liked it? You liked it last week.'

Orla raises a shoulder; she looks sidelong at Niall, who is shovelling in forkfuls, three at a go, before beginning to chew.

After tea, the kids go through to the sitting room, switch

on the TV. She scrapes Orla's bowl into the bin. She makes up two dishes of ice-cream and scatters them with sprinkles. Anything with calories. She texts Sean.

How are you getting on?

He texts back:

Paperwork. ☺ Home soon.

But shifts are like earthworms: they ooze and swell and stretch out longer than you'd think. She watches TV for a while with the kids, and then, when they go upstairs, she dumps her marking on the dining table and gets started. Orla can be heard getting ready for bed – bathroom door, taps, floorboards – but sounds from Niall's room – music, indecipherable speech, and then an explosion – suggest that he's on the PlayStation. Things gradually go still and quiet. She wades through her work. She takes off her glasses and rubs her eyes. There's a kind of disturbance at the edge of her vision, where there's something not quite right. A kind of shiver, an unshackling of one thing from the next. Migraine.

She closes her eyes, and the disturbance is gone. She opens them, and there it is again, in the corner of her sight. She turns towards it, but the disturbance doesn't move with her. It stays put on the patch of wall at the foot of the stairs. Then it closes up and blinks out.

This is not how migraines work.

Any idea when? ☺

Her phone screen fades out and goes black. He might

already be in the car. He might be turning down the street right now. Or he might be up to his elbows in someone. Or still shovelling his way through paperwork.

Light footfalls cross the landing and come down the stairs. Orla. She should have been asleep hours ago. She comes to a halt at the foot of the stairs, profile, in white nightie and fluffy socks, blonde plait hanging down her back. And now the disturbance is back, front and centre of Róisín's vision, but *behind* Orla; it shreds the wall, squirms and twists into itself, and is the door. It stands there, raw and out of kilter and just wrong. But right there, just on the other side of Orla.

Róisín is on her feet: 'Orla.'

No response.

'Come here, sweetheart, come here to me.' Róisín moves towards her. 'Please, Orla.'

But Orla turns away; she turns towards the wall. She reaches out and her hands fumble and feel their way, blindly slip through the structure of the door and slide over paper. Róisín lunges for her, grasps Orla's shoulders, pulls her round. The child is still sleeping; her blue eyes are wide open. And the door is gone.

'It's okay,' Róisín says, pulling her close, feels the child's heart thud against her. 'It's okay, it's okay.'

She steers Orla upstairs and gets her back to bed without waking her. She closes the door by degrees, wishes she could lock it. She creeps back down the stairs, rubbing at her arms, eye on the uneasy patch of wall. Temple pressed against the paper, she peers along its surface, slides her palm over it. The paper is flat and matte and cool. She feels a slight ridge when her hand passes from one sheet to the next, but that's all.

Migraine. Must have been a migraine. Or drifted off herself. Orla had sleepwalked. She'd muddled it together, imagined the rest.

She goes back to her work, but uneasily; she leaves the hall door open, so she can keep an eye on things. Nothing happens; Orla does not stir again. Róisín works her way through her marking. Every time she glances up, the wall is innocent and blank.

Then the front door is keyed open; she meets Sean in the hallway.

'Sorry I'm so late–' Seeing her expression, his face contracts: 'What's wrong?'

'Just. Orla was a bit unsettled tonight.'

He slumps. Not again.

'Sleepwalking, if you'll believe it. She came all the way downstairs.'

'Christ. Could have broken her neck.'

This hadn't even crossed her mind. She blanches, follows Sean upstairs; together they lean over Orla's bed. She is sleeping, pale and peaceful. Sean touches the back of his fingers to his daughter's cheek.

'Niall okay?'

She has no idea.

Niall is deeply asleep, sprawled face down and diagonally on top of his bed, the PlayStation controller and headphones lying on the floor where they've fallen. Sean folds the duvet up over him, switches off the screen and console, doesn't comment.

Sean microwaves his bowl of pasta; Róisín pours a glass of wine. They sit down across the table from each other. She chews her lip. She feels like she's on the verge of something: she could collapse into tears, or hysterics, or she could bolt for the door and just run away.

'That's just how she's wired,' Sean says. 'Try not to worry. She'll grow out of it. Eventually.'

'I don't know, I don't know.'

His creases deepen. 'What is it, love?'

'Not her. It's. I feel like I'm. Seeing things.'

He leans back, his professional hat on: 'Things. Like lights, colours, shapes, that kind of thing?'

'It looks like a door.'

She watches for his reaction; he raises his eyebrows, but that's it; the moment slips away: 'Any headache?'

She shakes her head.

'Could still be a migraine. Or maybe there's some damage to the retina. What's your blood pressure like?'

She has no idea. 'I just think I'm going a bit mad here, staring at the walls.'

He nods, considering this: 'Maybe we've outgrown the place?'

'The house? You think?'

'Well the kids have got big, but the house hasn't.' He gives her arm a squeeze. 'When we moved in it was just you and me.'

He smiles. She smiles too.

'I guess you just expand to fill the space you have. Shall we start looking?' he asks. 'Something with a bit more space?'

She leans across the table, and presses her lips to his lips.

'Any funny dreams last night?' she asks Orla in the morning.

Orla gives her one of her mercurial, sideways looks. 'Why?'

'You were sleepwalking. You came all the way down the stairs. Gave me the fright of my life.'

Orla's eyebrows raise: 'Don't remember.'

When Sean gets home from work that evening, he calls out a general hello but heads straight on up the stairs.

'What you up to?' Róisín follows him up.

'Just a thing. An idea.'

He heaves the attic ladder down and climbs up into the sooty dark. He thumps around awhile and emerges, dusty but triumphant, with the old stair gate tucked under an arm. He wipes it clean, then reinstalls it at the top of the stairs; electric drill and rawl plugs and everything. He opens and shuts it a few times, grins to Róisín:

Boom.

The next night, they are woken by the sound of rattling; it's a childproof latch; it needs a tricksy twist and slide and lift; Orla, sleeping, cannot work it loose. They hear her footfalls as she goes back to bed. And every night, until they move house in six months' time, Róisín hears the clack-clack-clack of sleeping hands fumbling with the gate. She stays alert, heart pounding, until the footsteps creak away.

It is half past four on a warm April afternoon and Róisín has been awake for twelve hours already. She's so tired her hands shake and her head is swimming. But she's happy. Moving around the new kitchen, plugging in the kettle, stowing crockery, she is still astonished at how much space they have. There's elbow room here, distance; they're no longer bundled together on top of each other. They own a lawn now. An actual apple tree.

She takes tea through to Sean, who's unpacking boxes in the living room. He extracts a mug from the bunch with a flinch – hot-hot-hot.

'You're a star.'

She flashes him a smile, then climbs the stairs. At last, a proper room for Orla. Space for a desk, a bookcase for her books, and a wardrobe, as well as her bed; they've given her the colourful old Habitat rug to soften the wooden floor. Orla, sitting like a pixie in the middle of the rug, is unpacking her books. She takes a mug in her thin hands.

'Happy?' Róisín asks.

Orla nods, sets the tea down, carries on with her books. She misses the old house; she didn't see why they had to move.

Niall has the attic rooms to himself; he is sprawled out on the oatmeal carpet, unravelling a web of black cables; he takes his mug, tells her he's sent her a link for that 72-inch telly he was telling her about; it would fit perfectly up here. She makes non-committal noises, leaves him to it.

Down one flight, in their new bedroom, she gazes out across the road, the railings, the empty playground, into the green sprawl of the park beyond. They haven't come far. If you stand at the end of their new street, you can see the old bakery, now turned into flats. But it feels like a miracle.

Her head see-saws with fatigue. She sets her mug down on the floor and lies back on the unmade bed. She blinks, drifts. Sean comes into the room, flumps down flat beside her.

'Missing the old place?'

She grins. 'Not one little bit.'

———

That last October, they wave goodbye to Orla at the airport. Their daughter is pale and determined, as is her nature, and Róisín is deliberately cheerful, right up until the moment when Orla turns the corner into Departures, and is gone. Eyes brimming, lips bitten, she holds it more or less together until they're in the car, where she collapses into sobs.

They sit in the carpark, Sean hugging her, his own eyes wet.

The house, when they get back to it, feels grey and hollow. Sean flicks on the central heating, switches on lamps, is his practical self. Orla will be fine. Róisín shouldn't worry. She'll be back at Christmas, she's not gone for good; who knows where she'll settle in the end, maybe just up the road like Niall; they should try and look on it positively. The family is not dispersing, but expanding.

He is right, of course. It will just take some getting used to. She opens a bottle of wine, pours them both a large glass, sets about making a lasagne. Sean switches on Radio 6, lays the kitchen table for two, throws together a salad, tidies up, refills her glass. They sit at the kitchen table and talk about everything else, and it's almost like it was before. But when she hefts the lasagne out of the oven and sets it on the table, she looks at it, then covers her face with the oven gloves, and bursts into tears.

'What? What is it, love?'

He strokes her shoulders. She shakes her head, sobs. 'Stupid.'

'What, though?'

She wafts the oven glove at the lasagne: 'It's too big. It's just stupidly, stupidly big.'

'It doesn't matter.' He rubs her shoulders a bit more, then gives her a proper hug. 'It's always better the next day, anyway.'

That night, she is walking through the house. The shadows are dusty grey curtains; she has to push her way through them. In the empty attic rooms a vast TV screen plays videogame footage; a desert track scrolls past rocks and scrubby trees and sandstone outcrops, towards a vanishing point, just up the road, that can never be reached. Then she is in Orla's room, which is also the box room from the old house, and a library. The walls are shelved from floor to ceiling in tea-coloured wood; Orla's bed is a cosy-looking little bunk on a lower shelf; her desk occupies a slightly higher one, with a Tiffany lamp and a chair drawn up to it; and over there is a library stepladder on wheels; and at the top of it, perched high up near the ceiling, Orla herself sits like an imp, so pale she is almost transparent, peering inquisitively down.

I thought you'd gone.

Orla looks at Róisín. Then she shakes her head.

Róisín wakes, washed through with happiness, but then tunes into the day, and remembers. Sean breathes softly beside her. A car passes in the road outside, a sound like a wave breaking. Sean is right, of course. He is practically, sensibly right. The family expands, moves outwards. It need not be a sadness or a loss; it's just what happens.

She pads down the stairs and into the kitchen, and it is only when she is standing there, waiting for the kettle to boil, that she realises what she just walked past. She goes back. Jammed in at the foot of the stairs, raw and out of kilter, is the door. She reaches out and touches it. A queasy give, like the skin on old paint. There's something thick and swollen and gone bad here. Open it and you don't know what might come seething out.

———————

In the doorway, her son is a hologram – at one angle there's the little boy he used to be, those soft hazel eyes and perfect gull-wing mouth – but then he turns to speak to little Finn, and she sees Sean in the shape of cheekbone and the widow's peak, and that's a whole other heartbreak. Finn, though, is an unmitigated joy. He rides on his father's forearm with the confidence of a king, holds out his plushy lion for grandma to admire; she takes the toy and shakes it back at him, growling. Finn hoots and claps.

'Come in, love.'

No hallway here. No staircase. Open plan. New build. It's a little raw around the edges; the front door opens directly into the living space; there's a kitchen in the corner; the bathroom and bedroom doors are jammed in just beside it. No messing around. Nothing wasted.

Niall sets Finn down on his feet, and the little boy runs off in joyous loops around the living room. Niall turns to his mother, to hook their smiles together.

'Doesn't have much room for that at home,' Niall says.

She pours milk into Finn's special sippy cup. Niall sits in

at the table, calls the boy over and lifts him on to his knee. He glances at the framed photograph on the wall beside him. They're in school uniform; he's grinning, adult teeth too big for his face. Orla, though, has just the ghost of a smile about her; an assessing, non-committal look. He turns away, but then glances back, buffeted around by pain and love.

They chat for a while. They take a few wobbly steps around the subject of Sean. The boy practises moving the cup from hand to hand, setting it down and picking it back up. Loss follows each of them around like shadows; when they come together, the shadows blend and blur and thicken, and make the loss even more exquisitely felt. Her eyes fill. She should be allowed this, at least. Son and grandson. A little peace.

Finn's sippy cup dangles forgotten from his fist; he's staring at her. She smiles for him.

'Don't you worry, my wee pet. Grandma's fine.'

Niall strokes the boy's hair. His jaw slides sideways. He shakes his head.

The only CCTV footage the police could find showed Orla marching past in her raincoat and winter boots, beanie pulled down over her blonde crop, headed in the direction of her flat. Her coat and keys and purse and passport were all found inside. There was no sign of a struggle. No valuables were missing. The police never found a body. But she hasn't been seen since.

'Do you remember the night terrors? The sleepwalking?' Niall asks.

'I'd hardly forget.'

'You know, back then, I was jealous.'

'Jealous?'

'It marked her out. It made her special.'

'I didn't want you to ever feel … I'm sorry if you felt …'

'Don't worry,' he says, though she can see that it's uncomfortable for him. 'I once asked her what it was like, you know.'

'She could never remember.'

'No, she did. She told me.'

She leans in: 'What did she say?'

'She was scared.'

'Well, duh.'

'Don't be like that, Mum.'

'Sorry. Okay. Scared?'

'She was afraid that she'd wake up and you'd be gone.'

'But I slept on her floor, night after night.'

'I'm just telling you what she said. I'm not saying it made sense. You were gone, and when she sleepwalked, she was going after you.'

Some kind of inward shift, a crack; something new and vulnerable and mollusc-like is pushing through. Then Finn thumps his cup down and sprays milk up into his face, splutters, wails. Distracted, Niall wipes him down, soothes him, then looks up and sees his mother's stricken face.

'Mum. *Mum*. Not your fault, honestly. What happened. Not Orla, not you and Dad. Seriously, none of it's your fault.'

'Okay. All right. Thank you, love. I'm all right. When did you say you needed to be off?'

The boys teeter down the front steps; she waves the car away and closes the front door. Then she turns to face the other door. She has been ignoring it ever since she first noticed it, a few months after moving in. It is jammed uncomfortably close to her front door. It is out of kilter, raw, but it seems far more at home now than it ever did before. Here everything else is also new and faintly out of true.

She lifts her phone to text Sean. She misses him; she misses his cheerful pragmatism, the way he'd see a problem and just fix it. It'd worked so well until it slammed up against a problem that could not be fixed.

Love you. Sorry.

She clicks her phone off, sets it down. They will find it in the empty, ordinary flat, along with her purse and coat and passport, and no sign of a struggle, when the police break down the door. It will show seven missed calls from Sean, who, when he sees the text from Róisín, and calls and calls and gets no reply, will race over in the car, lean on the doorbell and hammer on the door, alarming the neighbours, and getting no response at all from inside. He will then, for the first time in his life, dial 999, his hands shaking.

Now, though, the other door thrums and heaves in front of her, greyish-white and necrotic. She takes a breath and lets it go. This was always going to have happened; this was always waiting for her here. She feels an unwholesome, sick anticipation.

She grasps the handle; it pulses in her grip. She opens the door.

The Woman Who Let Go

Moyra Donaldson

CRAZY. Looking back, that's the only way I can describe myself in the weeks and months after Tom walked out. One moment I'd be so angry that I'd be fantasising about sticking a knife in him, the next I'd be curled up sobbing. The night he told me he was leaving, I'd been out at the opening of an exhibition, a young guy who'd just graduated with a First. I'd had a lovely evening – the gallery owner chatting to me about my own upcoming show, talking and laughing with friends. I'd drunk a little bit too much perhaps, but that's what people do on those sort of evenings. Everything was as it should be. When I got home, Tom was waiting up for me. He put the kettle on for coffee, asked me to sit down; he'd something to tell me. He had met someone else. I raged, I cried, I threw things, I was the very cliché of an abandoned wife, a woman destroyed. Thirty years of marriage, over. As far as Tom was concerned, I was relegated to the past – just like that. I was so humiliated, so hurt. Devastated. How could I not have seen it coming?

He wanted us to be *civilised* about it, he wanted to be fair to me, so I got the house. Fair – what a joke that was. All I could think about was getting rid of the damn place. I put it on the market as soon as I could and started looking for somewhere I could call my own, where there weren't piles of memories in every corner of every room, haunting me, lying around like faded wreaths on the grave of our marriage. Rosie thought selling up like that was madness – crazy. She'd phone from London and try, as she would put it, to talk some sense into me. But I was determined. I wanted somewhere to hide away, to be on my own and shut out the world. Tom had made a travesty of all I thought I knew. I'd been blown apart and needed to try to reassemble myself, though I couldn't imagine how my future would look.

From the moment I saw Ivy Cottage I knew that it was for me and that I could find peace there. The advertisement described it as a labourer's cottage, in need of updating, originally part of the Clandeboye Demesne. I just loved where it was situated, at the edge of the woods that surround the Big House and down a lane. Well away from the road. You couldn't even hear the sound of the traffic. Inside was just as perfect. As I walked through its rooms, the young estate agent followed behind me, prattling on, pointing out the Belfast sink and how I could knock down a wall, take out the old Rayburn, put in a wood burner and granite worktops. I wanted to tell her to shut up so that I could just take in the feeling. Even on that first viewing, the green light from the trees seemed special to me, full of magic.

Rosie took a couple of days' leave and flew over to have a look. I could tell she was getting a bit fed up with me. She was sympathetic of course, angry with her father, but she thought I should be 'pulling myself together'. She knew I was drinking most days and she thought the cottage was too isolated, that I'd regret it when I finally came to my senses. She thought I was making too hasty a decision. She didn't like the 'place', as she referred to it; found it dingy, claustrophobic, didn't like the way the trees cast their shade over the roof. Rosie likes big, bright rooms. She has no time for shade and subtlety. I love her very much, but she does take after her father; everything is clear-cut.

On the first morning in my new house, when I opened my eyes to its clean blessing, I thought I had awoken on the floor of a soft emerald ocean; the leaves sounded like waves when the breeze moved through them. I looked out at my dinky little garden full of old roses and felt my spirits lift.

Later that day, when I walked through the woods that surround my cottage, their beauty instantly took hold of me. It was spring and the bluebells were the sky brought down. Birdsong was the soprano note above the percussion of creaking branches, the mutterings of trees. I glimpsed a deer and her speckled fawn among the rhododendrons; those once imported and exotic plants that had escaped from the gardens of the Big House, turned native and run rampant over the years.

The sun bent its head to peer through and dapple the floor. I could feel a deep, ancient energy beneath my feet. For the first time in months I felt my body relax and my mind stop its constant obsessive circling round my pain. I sat down with my back against a tree and filled my lungs with good air.

I slept well that night and the next morning, I took a new canvas, took out my brushes and began to paint the green behind my eyes.

Later that evening, I started to get my belongings into place. I hadn't brought much from the old house, only essentials, so it didn't take long. Among the boxes was a package my old friend Sam had sent when he heard I was moving here. I hadn't got round to opening it, so when I unwrapped it, I was delighted to see a collection of old books. The note inside told me he'd picked them up in a second-hand bookshop and thought I might like them. Sam was always thoughtful; he'd once given me a piece of fulgurite for my birthday, a magical thing, formed when a lightning strike hits the ground, fusing silica to glass. I looked at the books, a RSPB publication about woodland birds and the wonderfully titled *Secret Life of Trees*. The third – *A History of Clandeboye and Its Surrounds*. When I went to bed, I took them with me to look through and discovered that there was evidence of Neolithic settlements in the area and that the O'Neills, who first owned the lands of

Clanaboy, were some of the most powerful people in Ulster in the 1500s. I read that the estate was first settled in 1674. In 1801, the Big House was built and in 1848, Frederick Lord Dufferin built the grand folly of Helen's Tower for his mother. I fell asleep thinking about time, the marks we leave on it. For the second night in a row, I slept well.

The next morning I walked to Helen's Tower at the crown of the woods. It rose through the surrounding trees and I could sense Belfast Lough to the north, Strangford Lough to the south. Scotland on the horizon. The Vikings that first sailed those waters must have looked up and seen this outcrop pushed up from the past. I imagined Comgall in Bangor Abbey, lifting his eyes to this ancient hill. I felt the same pulsating energy as I'd felt the day before, as if the ground itself had imbibed the history of the place. I felt as if all kinds of things could rise through it to meet my imagination.

A sudden memory came to me: on the train to Bangor as a child, passing through Helen's Bay, my father talking about how the village had been built by Lady Dufferin when the rail tracks were first laid; how the men of the 36th Ulster Division had been trained on the estate, prepared for the Western Front. *Got ready to be slaughtered*, he'd said. I remembered how his words had struck me at the time; it was unlike my father to speak like that, or to look so solemn. I shivered the memory away, but when I got back to the cottage, I looked to see if the soldiers were mentioned in my book. There they were, a few black and white photos of young men digging trenches, doing their military drills, or just posing for the camera. I felt the chill coming off them. Apparently it had been a cold, wet autumn and bitter winter, the grounds awash with mud when they billeted here, but in the photos, some of them are smiling; innocents, unaware of the horror that lay ahead.

I took the books to bed with me again and read of owls and wood warblers, root systems, and the early nineteenth-century mining of lead in the area. The minerals discovered there, galena and chalcopyrite, laid down on the sea bed and brought to the surface in the Triassic period. Apparently this is the only place in the North that you can find the mineral harmotome. The name delighted me and I laid the book on to the bedside table, turned off the lamp and fell asleep imagining the crystals vibrating in harmony with the trees.

I went deep into the woods every day. After breakfast and before I settled down in front of whatever canvas I was working on, I opened my little garden gate and entered the territory of trees. Of course other people walked there too, families with dogs, solitary walkers, all sorts. I avoided them, with their padded jackets and bobble hats, their loud voices and lack of respect. I resented their thoughtlessness, their trespass into my space. The trees resented them too. There was one young man though who seemed different, perhaps shy. I only saw him at a distance and he always turned away when he saw me, but I noticed how he sometimes laid his hands on to the trunk of a tree, stood as if listening. I sensed something damaged about him. I heard him whistle sometimes as he walked; a melody both jaunty and haunting. 'Johnny, I Hardly Knew Ye'. I named him for his tune.

―――――――

First time it happened, I was sitting in a quiet spot beneath a tree, allowing the peace to wash over me, when on impulse, I pressed my fingers through the layers of old leaves, into the earth beneath. I drew my hand back in surprise at the little electric shocks I felt in my fingertips. I pushed my fingers into the soil again. The same sensation. So it was that I connected to the life of the trees. I could sense the deep roots around the trunk and the roots spreading and intermingling with the roots of other trees, holding little objects from the past in their fingers; a sharpened flint, a brass button, a deer antler, a wolf tooth. Then the fine root tips joining with microscopic filaments of fungus. A symbiosis with the earth, with the history of the earth. That I was part of too. Nothing is separate.

I returned to my cottage, allowed this energy to flow out through my fingers, down the brush and on to the canvas.

I had cancelled my previous show and for a while the gallery owner emailed, wanting to rearrange, but I never replied and soon I didn't even bother going online to look.

I presume he stopped eventually. My old work held no interest for me; it seemed empty, all surface. I did not want to exhibit this new work which poured out of me every day. It was between me and the trees.

The winter passed like this. No matter the weather, nothing kept me from my daily commune with the trees. The stark sculpture of their leafless branches, the hieroglyphs of twigs written on winter skies, delighted me. Most days I'd see Johnny, always at a distance, always on his own, like me. On dark nights, I lay on my back and watched the planets travel their paths through the leafless canopy. Often I would hear a soft whistling, always that same tune, and I'd know that somewhere out there in the darkness, Johnny was watching with me.

————————

When spring came round again and everything was tipped in green and all the birds in a tizzy, I was so engrossed in this new way of seeing and being that I forgot all about Rosie coming over from London to see me. I was taken completely by surprise when she arrived at my door with her little wheelie suitcase and the cold air of the outside world about her. I admit I probably didn't create a good impression. My hair hadn't been cut in a year, or seen a colour. My fingers were thick with loam. I was dressed in an old jumper, covered in paint; the leaves and moss that I'd brought in for the painting

I was working on were scattered across the kitchen floor and the table was covered with bits of paper – my sketches of Johnny. I had been trying to capture his face. Dishes were piled up in the sink, stacks of canvasses leaning against walls. There wasn't much at all in the cupboards. I had started to find I wasn't very hungry – I was being sustained by the roots. Her concern showed on her face, but also her disapproval. On that first afternoon she went to the supermarket and came back laden with groceries.

She stayed two nights, but we didn't talk much. I found her irritating and tiring, asking about people I'd no interest in any more. Asking if I ever saw any of my old friends. Sighing as if I was a recalcitrant child. It was easier to just take myself out into the woods where Johnny was waiting, stay there most of the day. Rosie spent her days tidying and when I came back from my trips to the trees, she'd have food waiting for me that I'd pick at. I didn't want her to think I was ungrateful, but really I couldn't wait for her to leave again. I knew she thought I was still drinking, even though I'd told her it's not something I need any more.

On the evening before she left, we sat at the kitchen table. 'Mum,' she said, 'you haven't even noticed.' She waved her left hand under my nose. 'David and me got engaged, we're going to just have a small wedding in August. I really want you to come. I won't even invite Dad if you promise you'll be there. You can come over beforehand and we can go shopping, get you some new clothes, get your hair done.' I stared at the diamond glittering on her finger. I did feel bad at not having noticed, but it seemed like news coming from a different time, a different world that I was no longer part of. I couldn't care about it, though I knew I should. I could see how disappointed Rosie was with my reaction, so I did my best to look interested, I think I even managed to ask a few questions about her plans. She was a little tearful as she left. She hugged me tight and made me promise I'd think about coming.

Something changed again after Rosie's visit. There was an intensity in the air that made my heart beat faster, made me feel unsteady on my feet when I first rose in the mornings. I didn't feel right until I got out among the trees and steadied by their roots. The understanding came to me, flowing from the earth and through the xylem – the past was moving closer to me.

One unseasonably wet and blustery June night, under the sounds of the whipped branches and squalls of rain, I became aware of a soft, almost tentative knocking at my door. I was in bed, nearly asleep and in that floating, half-dream state. It took me a minute or two to register the sound for what it was rather than just a branch against the window. I got up, switched on the lamp and went to the door. No one was there, but I heard the sound of heavy boots, a rhythmical tattoo, echoing down the lane and into the darkness. Somewhere, out among the trees, an animal howled. I went back to bed and fell into sleep, back into dreaming. When I woke in the morning, I was shocked at myself, at just how explicit my dream had been. The sheets were tangled and damp, the air charged. Though I couldn't recall his face, I remembered his young body, his hunger for me. My hunger for him.

That afternoon, as I rested beneath my favourite chestnut tree, an agitation in the leaves, a pulsing hum in the roots, let me know that it was Johnny that had visited me last night. And would again. That I should be ready.

The weather had picked up, it was a warm evening, the birdsong was sweet and the trees sighed themselves into the late twilight. I lay awake, waiting, but I must have drifted off because I found myself jolted out of sleep by the creak of a loose board in the hallway. Something or someone was in the house. The door to my room opened slowly.

He stood framed in the doorway and though a peaked cap obscured his face I knew it was him, the whistler from the woods, the lover from my dream. I felt no fear. *Come in, Johnny*, I said quietly, and he moved closer. *Why don't you sit down?* I said, and he lowered himself wearily on to the edge of the bed and sat, his head in his hands. I touched his back and felt the heavy wool of his jacket, damp and smelling of the woods and the earth. I could also feel the exhaustion and sadness coming off him in great waves. I left my hand there and after a while I felt his shoulders begin to relax and he laid his hands on his knees. *Why don't you take off those heavy boots and rest a while?* I said. He bent down, undid the laces, swung his legs on to the bed and lay unmoving. I stroked his soft hair and heard his breathing grow slower. We lay like that, me under the duvet and him above it until we both fell asleep.

That was how it began. The need in me, calling through the years to the need in him. The trees heard us. Johnny doesn't talk much about the awful things he has been through, the things he has seen and done, though I know he will never forget. The trenches, the slaughter. I knew that the sight of Helen's Tower rising above the surrounding countryside was his last abiding memory of home before he departed for England and on to the Western Front. And this was where he came – after his battle was done and his body lay in the Flanders mud.

Rosie was very upset when I didn't make it to the wedding. I tried to explain, but I'm sorry now that I said anything about the trees, about Johnny. I've stopped answering her calls, stopped listening to the messages she leaves. There's no talking to her. She's threatening to come and I don't want her to. Her presence, her bright, logical mind – she'd destroy us. Johnny suggested I write, keep her away; he told me what to say:

Dear Rosie,

You may consider me crazy and you may not want to accept this, but I'm happy here. You don't need to worry about me and I don't want you to visit. Not all ghosts are to be feared.

Love to you as always – but please, just leave us in peace.

Mum

Now I'm free to do nothing but walk the woods with Johnny, listen to the trees and the earth and the layers beneath us. Hikers, families with dogs, pass us as if we're not even there. Each night we lie down together; we have made our bed in the fallen leaves and our legs and arms entwine amongst the roots, part of the great eternal network of the past. The trees brought us together; they have blessed us both, healed us both.

A Loss

Bernie McGill

IT'S hard to know what the truth of it is. I've been picking at a knot, but the looser it gets, the less I like what I see. Best to leave it as it is, maybe, though the impulse to keep worrying at it is difficult to withstand. 'The truth will out,' my aunt used to say to me as a boy, when she suspected me of keeping something from her, when I denied I'd been down to the boat slip again, begging the fishermen to take me out. As if truth were like oil and will rise to the surface; as if it will always declare itself in the end. It's the kind of idea that teachers and clerics used to terrorise us with in the past. It's the kind of idea I try to sell to my own pupils now, though we all know that they don't buy it. 'Truth is relative,' they say back to me. We're living in different times.

Aunt Sheila died September past, not long after the beginning of the new school term. She was my father's only sister. She lived just over an hour from where I live in the city, in a bungalow by the sea. She hadn't married, had taught in the grammar school in the town all of her professional life. She survived both my father and mother who passed away on the family farm, within a few months of each other, a little over a year ago. Aunt Sheila was in her late eighties and, as far as I knew, had lived in relatively good health up until a few weeks before her death when she had gone out one evening in her night clothes and suffered a fall on the sea path below her house. One of the neighbours had found her when they heard my aunt's little dog whining. I don't know what she was doing out there. I doubt that many people had seen her in her nightie before. She was a very correct sort of person, my aunt. She'd have been mortified if she'd known. As it turned out, she never regained consciousness. She'd suffered a severe contusion; must have knocked her head against the metal railing when she fell. The neighbour took the dog in at the time but wasn't keen to keep it. 'An animal's too much of a tie,' she had said.

The funeral was a quiet affair. I am my aunt's only surviving relative. A handful of uniformed school pupils, too young to have known her, formed a guard of honour at the church door; a few older parishioners, former colleagues and ex-pupils followed the cortège to the outskirts of town. She was buried in a plot she had picked out for herself in the corner of the graveyard. Afterwards, in the parish hall, over tea and a medley of sandwiches, I fielded handshakes and condolences while former pupils reminisced about their school days, told me what a dedicated teacher Aunt Sheila had been, how much she would be missed.

I hadn't visited my aunt much in recent years. My clearest memories of the place were from the seventies, the summer I was sent to stay with her. I had asthma as a child and suffered at hay-making time. My father had taken it into his head that a stay by the sea would clear my lungs. I remember sitting in the front seat of the Cortina beside him, driving down the hill to her house, the first sight of the sea, the gulls wheeling, screeching overhead, the bag nets strung up along the shore, drying in the sun. My mother didn't come with us. There had always been some tension between the two women. I wonder if my mother was a little envious of what she used to call my aunt's 'independence'. The way she said it sounded pejorative, like the word she meant to use was 'selfishness'. But my father was very fond of his sister. You could see that in the way they spoke together. That visit, he brought her a bag of early spuds from the farm, a clutch of fresh eggs. 'Those'll put a bit of colour back in your cheeks,' he said.

I spent hours down at the boat slip that summer, bare-footed in the shallow water, fishing in the rock pools for hermit crabs and shrimp, watching the fishermen set out to haul in the bag net, waiting for them to come back in with the catch. My aunt forbade me to go out with them, said the sea was too dangerous, unpredictable for a farm boy like me. There was one man, Bill, who used to deliver fish to her and who provided, since my aunt didn't drive, a makeshift taxi service from time to time. They were friends of sorts. I thought, if I kept on at Bill, that he would relent and take me out in the boat. I used to wait for him near the ice house. He would often stop by there to pick up some fishing gear on the way out, but he wouldn't defy my aunt. 'Miss Scullion would have my guts for garters,' he used to say, and then laugh, as if he were picturing what that might look like. I remember him that summer I was there, in his flat cap, ears that stuck out like jug handles either side of his head, carrying a silver salmon up to her door. I remember Aunt Sheila in the pantry preparing the fish with a vicious-looking wooden-handled blade, slicing the scales off its back in one long strip. She was never squeamish. She'd grown up on the farm, helping my grandfather birth lambs before my father was old enough to help, before she went off to college. She didn't visit us much in the country, though Bill would drive her down now and again, and occasionally bring something for the septic tank.

The septic tank on the farm gave us trouble when it overflowed and waste from the house seeped into the lower meadow. A builder had told my father that if he dropped the carcass of a dead animal in from time to time, that it would resolve the issue. I've heard this again since: it's something to do with enzymes breaking down matter, speeding up the process of decomposition. Some people swear that it works.

When the tank overflowed, my father kept a lookout for a fox or a badger killed on the road, or a stillborn lamb in the spring. The fishermen near my aunt would sometimes find dead seal cubs on the rocks in the autumn, and Bill said, if the timing was right, he would bring one down when they came. The last day they drove down to the farm, some weeks after the summer I'd spent with her, Sheila and my mother had a bit of a falling out. I remember my mother restacking the unused china after Sheila and Bill had left, clattering everything back into the cabinet in the parlour. 'Wouldn't put a foot over the threshold,' she said, 'not even for a sup of tea. The face on her. You'd think it would have poisoned her. The place where she was born. Not good enough any more for the likes of her.' I could see that the rift had saddened my father, though he didn't say much at the time. My father was a quiet man, content at his work, the round of his life dictated by the turning of the seasons, the demands of the land. When it came to a battle of words, there was no winning against my mother.

A few weeks after my aunt's funeral, during the October half term, I drove back down to the coast to sort out things at her house. As soon as my car pulled into the drive, the next-door neighbour appeared, only too glad to pass my aunt's dog back to me. 'Sheila was a good neighbour,' she said. 'She never gave us any bother, but she was getting a bit confused. Seemed to always be out on the sea path lately, looking for something

she thought she'd lost. I hope she's at peace now.' I thanked
her and took the dog.

It was a nervous little beast, a cross of some kind, brown
and white, low-bellied, a touch of the foxhound about its face.
Once inside, it sniffed around, circled its bed in the alcove
beside the hearth, settled down with its chin on its paws and
eyed me with suspicion. At that time I had some notion of
keeping the dog. A city flat is not an ideal home for a pet, but
I was thinking that at some point I might take early retirement,
fix up the old farm house, settle back at home. The fields are
nearly all leased out, but for a while I had a vision of myself
as a gentleman farmer, strolling down to the lower meadow of
a summer evening, listening out for the call of the curlew the
way my father used to do, the small dog at my heels.

It was one of those dry, still days at the coast, just after
the clocks go back, when it feels as if the season is holding
its breath, readying itself for winter. The house was cold. I set
a fire in the hearth. The place was full of furniture for which
I had no use. The agents had said they'd deal with everything
but I didn't want to leave any personal papers lying around –
I had that much of my mother's circumspection in me, and
something, I suppose, of her acquisitive nature. If she'd been
alive, she would have directed me to check for any valuables
that had been stashed away. The house was coming down
with old schoolbooks, knitting patterns and recipes torn
from magazines, novenas and relics stacked on armchairs and

side tables near her bed. She'd got into the habit of jotting down anything that caught her attention off the television or the radio. On the backs of envelopes and in the margins of newspapers I found little snatches of writing in blue biro: song titles; a few lines of a prayer; the date the *Titanic* was lost; the name of a man in Sligo who had the cure for impetigo; the correct way to spatchcock a chicken. Marginalia and glosses that had importance only for her. I stuffed fistfuls of paper into bags to empty into the recycling bin. I kept a few old photos of her and Dad, one black and white snap of the two of them, dressed for Holy Communion or Confirmation, hands joined in prayer. Aunt Sheila, serious-faced, looking into the camera lens, Dad peering up, taking the cue of solemnity from her. Everything else, postcards and addressed bills, I dropped into the flames.

I was surprised to find from the agents that my aunt's estate included the ice house; she must have lent or leased it out to Bill. An old stone building, less than a quarter of a mile from the house, right on the shore facing the now disused boat slip, it was built into a lump of basalt that towered over the rear of the building. One small, high, boarded-up window looks out towards the sea. At some point a brick chimney was added to the landward side. The building was to be sold along with the bungalow. I decided to have a look to see if there was anything of interest in there.

I found the dog's lead on a hook by the back door. As soon

as I picked it up the animal began to bound around the room. I locked up and headed for the steps that lead down to the sea path. The ice house is to the north, in the direction of the town, I could see its single chimney from the road, but the dog had other ideas. As soon as we emerged on to the path she tugged on the lead in the direction of the beach. I followed her, decided to leave the ice house till later. I suspected she hadn't had much exercise in the weeks before. She seemed to know where she wanted to go.

There was hardly a breath of air, the sea as flat as a mill pond, just a curl of white surf showing. The dog padded along the path and headed to a small sandy inlet just before the main strand, a spot known previously as the Gentlemen's Bathing Place. My aunt used to say that no matter what went in the water to the north, it would wash up back there. I unhooked the lead and the dog dashed down the steps to where a culverted waterway emerged from a concrete pipe, spilled over some rocks and down into the sea. She nosed around the shore, snuffling under bladderwrack and beach debris, began to tug at something that was tangled up in weed until she emerged with a pale stump, that for a split moment, I took for bone. She ran back to deposit the thing at my feet. It was a piece of driftwood, stripped of bark, light, friable, in my hand. I threw it for her and half an hour passed, as I patrolled the shoreline, and the dog chased the stick in and out of the sea. Then I hooked the lead on to her collar and headed back in the direction of the ice house. As we climbed the steps from the beach back up on to the path, I felt the air grow damp and when I looked to where we were walking, I saw that a mist had begun to creep in from the sea. It was growing dark now. There are no street lights on the path, but at certain points pools of yellow light spill over from the road above. The mist thickened as I walked, diffusing the light, making it difficult to see ahead.

I was rounding a bend, not far from the ice house, when the dog stopped short and pulled to the seaward edge of the path. I couldn't see anything that would have caused her to cower. I tugged on her lead but she whimpered, refused to budge. I stepped closer to her to shorten the lead, leant for a moment against the metal railing that borders the path, and it was then that I felt a vibration, a low thrum, as if something – or someone – was knocking against it. The legs of the railing are set in the cement of the path. The dog must have felt the tremor in her feet. As I stood there, the vibration strengthened. I tugged on her lead again and a low growl grew in her. There was nothing to do but to pick her up. For a small dog, she wasn't light. Her feet and belly were wet from the sea. I took a few steps forward on the path, but as I walked towards the blind corner, she began to twist and claw at me, digging her nails into my arm, whining all the time. I swore and dropped her. The dog landed on her feet and bolted back along the way we'd come, the handle of the lead bouncing along the path behind her. I felt a damp patch on my sweater, too warm to be sea water, realised the dog had pissed on me. I retraced my steps towards the beach, calling for her, all the while cursing the fog and the dark and the damp seeping through to my skin. There was no sign of her on the small beach, or on the main strand. I walked up the path to the lights of the golf club and returned to the house by the road. When I reached it, I found the dog shivering on the doorstep.

My aunt had been teetotal, but in a cupboard in the pantry I found an unopened half-bottle of whiskey, stored away, no doubt, for one of those recipes she'd collected, a Christmas cake that she never got around to baking. I helped myself to a glass or two. That night I lay in the bedroom I'd slept in on my visit as a boy, with the window on the latch, listening to the dull lap of the sea. I read for a while from one of the magazines that lay around, an uninspiring article on the benefits of walking, and then I fell asleep, unused to the narrow bed, with my knee and my hand hanging over the side. At some stage during the night, I became aware of a draught of air in the room, and I rose and closed the window, fell back into an uneasy sleep.

I woke, stiff and cramped, in the morning, with a headache and with a foul taste in my mouth, and walked into town to clear my head, leaving the dog where it was. I ate a hearty breakfast of eggs and soda bread, flicked through a newspaper, and then headed back to the house by the sea path, calling at the ice house on the way. There is only one entrance to the building, a weather-beaten door gained via a steep gravel slope to the landward side. The padlock was rusted, silted with sea air; the place had been locked up for years, but the agents must have already tried the lock, and with a bit of effort I got the key to work. It was bitter cold in there, despite the mild October weather. The walls must have been up to three feet thick in places: you couldn't hear a sound from within. The interior was brick-clad, had been used, I believe, to store fish at a time when the shore was still used for draft netting. There was no evidence of a power supply. A hurricane lamp sat rusting by the door. Cobwebs hung in festoons from the rafters. As I stepped across the floor, something scuttled in the dark. With the light on my phone, I made out a tangle of nets, a number of discarded lobster pots, a few rusted tins of paint. And in the corner, on a mildewed, stained mattress, some tattered rags that could once have been bedding, which looked as if they hadn't been disturbed for years. Maybe someone had kept a dog or a cat in there, though the creature would have had to be let in and out since the door, as far as I remembered it, was kept locked from the outside. And it would have been a cold and a dark and a miserable bed with the high window boarded up as it had been for as long as I'd known the place. It was dry inside. That's all that could be said in its favour.

I locked up and went back to the house, relit the fire and

returned to my task. My aunt, in her later years, had taken to knitting what my mother used to call 'matinée jackets' for babies: little open-weave affairs, always in pale blue, with tiny pearlised buttons and ribbons. More decorative than practical, my mother liked to say: the work of a woman who knew nothing of the messy business of motherhood. Aunt Sheila shipped them off, every now and again, to the Good Shepherds in the city. 'It's something to occupy my hands,' she would say, 'and my head.' One drawer of the chest in her bedroom was full of them. I unpacked the small garments into bags for the charity shop. I didn't have much time.

I dampened down the ashes of the fire and raked them through the grate, filled the back seat of the car with bags, put the dog and its bed in the boot and left. I pulled up at the charity shop in the town, just before it closed for the day. As I pulled the bags out of the car, a scrap of paper fell out, a few lines of something in my aunt's distinctive copperplate handwriting that could have been part of a rhyme, or a song, or something she had composed herself. I folded it into my trousers pocket and carried on with my task. Back in the flat that night, I pulled out the scrap of paper, unfolded it, and sat down on the edge of the bed to read. It was only a few words, the lines from a skipping rhyme, remembered from her childhood, or heard, perhaps, in her teaching years: 'Miss Lucy had a baby, she called him Tiny Tim. She put him in the bathtub to see if he could swim.' I'd heard the younger girls at school sing a version of the rhyme myself, but something about seeing the words in my aunt's own handwriting gave me pause. I thought again of that mattress in the ice house, of the cold and the quiet in there. And then I thought of that last day that Aunt Sheila and Bill had come to the farm, to sort out the problem with the septic tank.

The day the car arrived in the yard, we all went out to meet it. My mother said to Bill and my father to head on down to the lower meadow and she would put the kettle on. Bill hauled an old, stained sack out of the boot of the car. Aunt Sheila sat in the passenger seat and wound down the window. She said she had been a bit car sick, that she wouldn't bother coming in. My mother said a gulp of tea would do her good: 'Tell her,' she said to my father. 'You wouldn't surely drive all the way back without taking something?' But my aunt wasn't for budging. I turned my attention to Bill. I'd never seen a seal cub before.

'Was it born in the sea?' I asked him.

'What?' Bill said.

'The baby seal.'

'No,' he said. 'No, they birth on land.'

'What happened to it?' I asked.

'It's hard to say,' Bill said, and looked to my father who was talking in the car window to Aunt Sheila.

'Come on out o' that,' said my father, 'and let the man get on.'

'Can I see?' I asked Bill.

Aunt Sheila turned sharply towards me at that and, in unison with Bill and my father, said 'No.'

Bill heaved the sack on to his back.

I wanted to go with them, but my mother said the septic tank was no place for a child. I watched my father and Bill walk down the well pad towards the marshy ground, the slight weight of the sack on Bill's back, a shape in it that a small round head might make. And then my mother said that whatever about the rest of them, she wasn't going to conduct her business in the street, and she marched back to the house and called after her for me to come in. I looked at Aunt Sheila. She was paler than the last time I'd seen her, thinner too. I suppose she'd have been about forty then. She was staring after Bill and my father with a stricken look on her face, like she wished she could will them to stop with her eyes. And then my mother called me again and I had to go. I was never sent to stay with Aunt Sheila again after that.

I kept the dog in the flat for a night or two and then dropped it at an animal shelter. The neighbour was right: a dog's too much of a tie. My aunt's house was sold, the ice house along with it. I paid off the mortgage on my flat. I won't fix up the farmhouse now. I'll stay in the city where I have no history, where I can walk the streets in peace. I think of my aunt often, and wonder about her, and about the words that she wrote on that scrap of paper, words that must have been long in her head. And I marvel, not for the first time, at the secrets people keep, for themselves, and for others, at the sadnesses that betray them, and at the small quiet lives that they continue to live out until the end of their days.

The Leaving Place

Jan Carson

I should have left the children with my sister. They are too young. Later, when they are older, they will remember this afternoon and wonder if they ruined it for you.

You want to say goodbye at home. It would be easier for you. For them. For all of us. But I'm thinking about the drive from the forest back to our house. How empty the car will feel without you; how light and empty. I'll need the children to pin me down.

In the car, on the way to the forest, the children are their usual demanding selves. Anna asks if we can have McDonald's for dinner. Fergus says McDonald's is disgusting. He's seen, on telly, that their chicken nuggets are made of liquidised feet. Anna hits Fergus. Fergus hits back harder. He is five. She's only three. In the resulting kerfuffle, milk is spilled. The sour stink of it will linger in the car for weeks, bitter and familiar as the memory of this afternoon.

Alarmed by the racket, the baby wakes and begins to howl.

He can't be pacified. I try everything. Soft, soothing words. Reaching behind myself to pat him one-handed on the knee. Raisins. I even give him chocolate buttons, though in the list of rules you've left behind, chocolate's only to be administered as a special treat. (You have not even gone, and I am already failing.) In desperation I put on his nursery rhymes CD and crank up the volume. The children are still yelling, but it is harder to hear the specifics through a solid wall of Old MacDonald and his farmyard friends.

'I'm sorry,' I say. 'This isn't how we planned it.'

I'd intended to give you Joni Mitchell at the end, a freshly valeted car and calm, smiling children: clean and well-presented, like children lifted from the *Next* catalogue.

You'd wanted it not to be raining for once.

You are more of a realist than me.

'Never mind,' you say. 'The kids are just being themselves. It makes it more normal.'

'Normal?' I say. 'Normal's the last word I'd use for today.'

You try to smile but it's too painful. Everything is painful now. Talking. Not talking. Even sleeping hurts. You haven't taken your tablets since yesterday morning. You want to be present at the end. You say the tablets blur the edges so you don't know where your own body begins and ends.

I lay my hand lightly on yours. Your skin is petal-like and bruised from all the times they've tried to slide the drip in and missed and tried again. Your whole hand disappears beneath mine. I was prepared for the sickness and the pale, yellow shade your face would turn, the clouds of hair appearing like tiny, drowned creatures, in the shower basin. I'd seen all this in films. I was not prepared for the way you'd shrink. The treatment has taken so much of you. When I carry you through the forest it will be like carrying a child. Fergus weighs more than you and he is small for his age, slight and willowy like a maple sapling.

The car park is empty. At least we will have privacy.

I get Fergus and Anna out of the back seat and usher them round to the passenger door. It's lashing now and I haven't thought to bring an umbrella. The children are itching to get back into the dry. Everything's rushed because of the rain.

You take your time. You lay your hand on each child's head. You are solemn in your blessing. 'Mummy loves you so much,' you say. 'Be brave. Be kind. Look after your daddy.' I don't know where your strong voice is coming from. You are like an unbroken line with our children.

I hold the baby for you. You're too weak to lift him yourself. You kiss the crown of his head where the hair's worn away. You breathe in his powdered baby smell. As I lift him away, you look straight at me and do not blink. Your eyes are beginning to swim. I understand now that I am being selfish. It is too much to ask of you; parting like this, in a rainy car park.

I will the children to say something meaningful. Surely,

Fergus is old enough to sense the mood. *I love you, Mummy* would be ideal. Instead, he says, 'It's raining. Can I get back in the car?' Anna is on the other side of the car park toeing the edge of a mucky puddle. I wish, in this minute, our children were different children. Only the baby is playing along.

We've agreed not to scare them. I'm not going to say, *This is it, kids, Mummy's never coming back*, but I feel like some sort of benediction's necessary. They might hold this moment against me for the rest of their lives.

'Mummy's going away for a while,' I say, raising my voice so Anna can hear. 'Come and say goodbye.'

'If Mummy's away can we get McDonald's for dinner?' shouts Anna, bolting across the car park. 'Can we go through the drive-thru?'

'No,' I snap.

'Why not?'

'Because the chicken nuggets are made out of feet,' says Fergus.

I can't believe this is your last precious moment with your children. I don't know how to make it better.

'Get in the car,' I say.

I buckle the baby into his stiff-backed seat. I tell Anna and Fergus to behave themselves for a change. 'Mummy and I are going for a wee walk,' I say. 'I'll be back in five minutes.'

'Are you going to do kissing?' asks Anna. She's only just realised that adults kiss differently from children.

'Yes,' I say, 'we're going to do grown-up kissing on our own.'

Anna smiles. Fergus makes a puking face. This seems as good a place as any to make our exit. I leave the nursery rhymes playing. I give Fergus raisins for the baby and a dummy in case he starts fussing. I lift you out of the passenger seat, gently, gently as if you are made of spun glass. I carry you across the car park, into the forest, turning my whole body so you can catch the last glimpse of your children's faces furring through the steamy windows.

'Look at what we made together,' I say. 'Aren't they beautiful?'

I have rehearsed these words on the drive over. They are the right words, but Fergus is ruining them, pressing his face against the glass so his nostrils flare and his mouth looms open like a wide fish mouth. He is wiping his slabbers across the window.

'Lock the doors,' you whisper. 'I don't want anything getting at my babies.'

I fumble for the clicker. It's not in my pocket. The keys are still hanging from the ignition. I make a pretence of pressing it. You are too tired to notice the doors don't lock. You believe your children are safe in the car. You would not leave them otherwise.

I find the entrance exactly where they said it would be. There's a green ribbon tied around a tree trunk. It's not an official path. The grass has been trampled down, then scuffed back up to disguise the entrance. You wouldn't want anyone stumbling into the clearing. It's a space reserved for those who need it.

I turn sideways, edging us past the brambles. Your face presses into the hollow of my neck. Your legs are like wet washing, draped over my arm. These last few months I've carried you so many times. From the bedroom to the couch. From the couch to the car. From the car to a wheelchair and, from there, to a bed in a white, white room with no windows and a chemical smell. Each time it has taken less strength to lift you. We've made a joke of it. You aren't losing weight. I'm growing stronger from all this lifting. Power lifting, you call it. You say I should be paying you for the work out.

Today, you are lighter than ever, and I can hardly bear the weight of it.

The light leaves us in shades. It is darker than I'd anticipated. I wish I'd brought a proper torch. The path is damp. The air, sullen. The rain, filtering through the trees, sounds faint and freckled like a distant stream. We do not speak to each other. There is nothing left to say.

I use the light on my mobile to pick out the ribbons. Everything's green in here, but the ribbons are a more demanding shade. Someone has taken the time to measure them and cut them and tie each one carefully to the trunk of a tree, marking a path through the forest. I am grateful for this kindness. We've been told to look for the ribbons and, just before the clearing, a small, stagnant stream which marks

the l   As we approach it, the
darki   le of light, like a watery
blue   rain holds its breath for
a whe

I s   iddle of the Leaving Place.
'Is   ar breath is barely strong
enoug
'Tl
Th   .
It's   eaming it. I wonder if you've
dream   reedy grass. The trees like tall
soldier   eter. The flat stone laid in the
centre,   size of a tipped headstone. I will
leave y   er's blanket tucked around your
should   getting cold.
Thi   uite differently. In the hospital,
with machines and lesser pain. At home, in the living room,
held together by a hospice nurse. In the bath, as we'd initially
planned, all warmth and candles, a handful of hoarded tablets
washed down with our wedding malt. I wanted to go with
the easiest option; the one which would involve least pain.
In the end, it was not my decision to make. It wasn't even
a negotiated thing like choosing a house or a baby name.

You insisted upon the Leaving Place.

You said it felt natural; traditional even. Leaving ran
through your family like a passed-down tea set. Your

grandmother – crippled by cancer of the bone – had begged to be left in the forest. Your grandmother's mother went similarly. She'd had something swelling in her brain: a kind of tumour, which took her sight and left her head so screaming sore, they'd called it kindness to carry her out to the Leaving Place. There are already plans for your father. He'll leave next year or the one after. It depends how quickly the dementia takes hold.

At first, I was adamant. I would not be leaving you in a forest. I did not care how natural it felt; how the trees would take care of you. I grew up in a sort of city. I knew nothing of the country or its odd ways.

You persisted. You were calm throughout; calmly determined.

'I'll do whatever it takes,' I said, 'but please don't ask me to leave you.'

You said you needed me to leave you. You couldn't manage it alone. The pain had stripped the pith right out of you.

'Please,' you said, over and over again, night and day, for almost a week until your insistence turned me thin and I said, 'Yes, I will leave you,' though I didn't know if I actually could.

Then, we began to make plans.

How I would raise our children in your image.

How I would not leave it too long – two years at most – before beginning to see other women. How I would judge these women on their own merits, not their similarity to you.

How I'd explain your end to the various interested parties:

doctors, not-so-close friends, our children, who were too young for anything but a moderated version of events.

How you wanted the leaving to be.

I am following your instructions carefully. It is the only thing you've asked of me.

I lay you out on the central stone, tucking the blanket around your shoulders and toes. I kiss you once on the lips. I close your eyes like you're already gone. I do not say the word goodbye. You've been clear on this; no goodbyes, no hysterics. Instead, I say, 'You have been so very loved.' I leave the swell of this hanging over you like a burnt offering.

I turn and walk away from the Leaving Place. I do not look back. You haven't stipulated this, but I know myself too well. If I look back, I will see you, small and defenceless with the trees already reaching down. I won't be able to leave you there. I won't be able to walk away.

I walk away, following the green ribbons in reverse. I do not cry. We've agreed upon this. I have to be strong for the children's sake. Late at night, when the three of them were fast asleep, you'd make me practise not crying: 'Think of never seeing me again,' you'd whisper. 'Hold that thought until it stings. Don't let yourself cry.' If you caught me crying – or even tearing up a little – you'd pinch me hard. You'd gather a crease of soft flesh between your thumb and finger and nip until you left crescent-shaped indentations like parentheses running the length of my arms. If I had to cry, I could do it in private.

Never, ever in front of the kids. You were not to be shifted on this point. Your nails remained sharp, right to the end.

When I reach the car park's edge I pause for a moment, feet straddling the line where the forest ends. Everything is different now, yet here is the car, sitting exactly where we left it, and there are our children, blurring pinkly through the foggy windows. They will require feeding and cleaning and every other ordinary thing. I settle my voice. I think my words straight. I will say, 'Mummy's gone to get a bit of peace and quiet. I'll come back and get her later.' I will say this in my best dad voice.

Best dad voice goes out the window the second I arrive at the car. The baby's in his seat, howling. Anna's making her way through the remains of the chocolate buttons. Fergus is nowhere to be seen.

'Where's Fergus?' I say, my voice shrill and climbing.

'He went to find you and Mummy,' says Anna.

I am howling like the baby. I am making sounds instead of words. Anna is rigid with fear. She's clinging to her seatbelt like it is a rope she might climb to get out of here. Her daddy's making a monster noise. Her mummy's left her alone with him. It must be awful in her head, like she's wandered into a story book world. I should stay and comfort my daughter, but I can't leave Fergus in the forest alone.

'Stay in the car,' I say. 'Don't move. I'm going to find Fergus.'

I can hear Anna wailing as I sprint across the car park. The baby raises his voice to harmonise. I'm torn between them and the forest beyond. You'd warned me it would be like this. 'You'll be pulled all roads and directions,' you said. 'You'll always feel like you're failing them.' You'd a smile on your face when we had this chat as if you were recalling a particularly fond memory: a birthday party or a romantic meal.

Fergus won't answer when I call for him. It will take almost fifteen minutes of searching before I find him, sitting on an old fir stump just inside the Leaving Place. He won't be panicking or crying, just staring at the branches above his head, swaying with them, as if he's hypnotised. I will run to him. I will pick him up. I will carry him quickly out of the forest, through clawing brambles and mulch-thick mud. All the time I will be talking. I will be challenging the hungry silence. 'Sorry, sorry, sorry,' I will say. 'Are you okay? I'm so sorry.' Fergus won't speak. He'll hold himself stiffly in my arms like the branch of a tree, or a boy who's seen more than he should have.

I will set him down on the car park's edge, placing his feet on the firm tarmac. I will go over him carefully looking for signs. The skin on his face will seem paler than usual. I'll raise my own hand for contrast and wonder if the shade is slightly green and if his eyes, which were always hazel, are a little more mossy than the last time I looked. I will pick the leaves from his hair, the twigs and prickly needles. I will wipe the mud stains off his arms. I will say very loudly in a confident voice, 'Look at the state you've got yourself in,' because this is a normal kind of thing to say when your child's been playing in a forest. I will try to ignore the silence in him.

Tomorrow, when I return for you, I will leave the children with my sister. I will warn her that Fergus isn't himself at the minute. 'It's his mother,' I'll say, 'he knows something's wrong.' I won't mention his silence or the pale green rash mottling over his lower legs. Sure, you'd only see it if you were looking for it. It's probably just a reaction to the washing powder.

I will drive to the forest on my own. With no one there to disappoint, I will allow myself to cry. I will follow the ribbons back to the Leaving Place and find you, exactly where I laid you: still and quiet, swaddled in a blanket of leaves. I will peel pack the fine branches which have fingered their way across your face and sever the roots that bind you to the ground. You will be pale and glowing in the muggy light as I close your eyes for the final time. I will note your lips raised in an almost smile. I will choose to believe the trees are kind.

I will carry you back to the car; belt you in like you're still alive. I will talk without ceasing all the way home. This and that and nothing specific. I will keep my eyes glued to the road. If I don't stop talking, I won't hear your silence. If I don't look at you, in the real-world light, I won't see the pale, green glooming of your skin. And I won't be reminded of our little boy. I will not be afraid that he's leaving me too.

Bird. Spirit. Land.

Ian McDonald

*'A fire is burning in Bird Spirit Land. My bones smoulder.
I must journey there.'*
Robert Holdstock, *Lavondyss*

SHE hid from the wings in the chimney until they
stopped beating. The house was small but full of leftover
histories. Old gas pipes that leaked the smell of onions when
the wind blew from the east. Mounting blocks and boot
scrapers from its time as the lodge of a grand house, long
fallen. Lost flues from the coal age, sealed inside boxed-in
chimney breasts. Into which a bird – a magpie, Ria guessed
from the rattling cries – had fallen.

It took her some time to trace the thrashing to its source
in her living room, but she couldn't open the chimney breast
and the landlord was not prepared to waste money rescuing
a magpie. By the second morning she could no longer bear
the flapping and croaking and moved television and laptop

into the kitchen. She closed the door on the walled-up bird but muttered an apology each time she passed on her way to bedroom or bathroom. She entertained a fantasy of pouring boiling water down the flue to end it quickly, but she was not sure it would do that, and she had no way to get up on the roof.

Each morning she cracked open the living room door and listened for a rustle, for a failing wing-beat. It took four days. Longer than she thought a bird could live in a six-centimetre flue. In the soot. In the dark.

She waited a day more before moving back into the living room. There was nothing she could have done. Nothing anyone could have done. Long after it was surely dead she imagined the fluttering of a soot-caked bird mummifying inside her wall.

———

When she first came to care for Mrs Fogel she hated the paintings. She hated the house, the curtains pulled to keep out the treacherous sunlight. She hated the job: cooking meals, giving baths, changing bags. Mostly she hated the paintings: so big, so many, so looming, so full of images that made her feel uncomfortable. Women becoming birds becoming sprays of stars or plants or rainbow-fringed things for which she had no names.

'What are they meant to be?' she asked, holding the old

woman's hand, which she loved, as she rode the stairlift down
to the studio.

'They're not meant to be anything,' Mrs Fogel said. Ria
helped her into the walking frame. 'A painting is.'

'But what are they *of*?'

The old woman clapped her hands, thin and creased
as origami.

'That is the question!' she said. 'They are of Bird
Spirit Land.'

Installed in her studio, Mrs Fogel needed little supervision.
Resented it, so Ria skipped out half-days for coffee, gym, a nip
to the shops. The timetable was: feeds; the arrival of Joanne
on the night shift; the capacity of the catheter and colostomy
bags. But in the end Ria's timings failed, the Zimmer frame
failed, the studio failed. Mrs Fogel asked Ria to lay out her
paints in an invariant order and tape the brushes to her wrists.
Ria now was forced to stay in the studio as the old woman
could not move the wheelchair with the brushes spiking from
the backs of her hands.

Like Wolverine, Ria thought, then that glib image was
eclipsed by the sick fascination of Mrs Fogel's hands pecking
at the canvas. Whole afternoons to stab a patch of colour
the size of a banknote. Ria watched Mrs Fogel struggle, Mrs
Fogel fail.

She had been a painter of note, Ria read, of the generation
of Basil Blackshaw, Neil Shawcross, Deborah Brown – names

that meant nothing to Ria. Anna Fogel studied Fine Art at York Street, but a meeting with Rowel Friers encouraged her toward illustration. She produced a compendium of Ulster birds in watercolour, collected in *Bird-life of the North*. Book and individual prints were highly sought-after. In the late sixties, she returned to fine art and gained attention through her *Murmuration* series, monumental canvases that sought to capture the starling flocks that flew every evening over the Waterworks opposite her home on the Cavehill Road. The motion of birds drew her eye deeper. Throughout the seventies she produced canvas after canvas of surreal, otherworldly images of a realm she called Bird Spirit Land. The market rejected such starkly personal work, but it appealed to the fledgling Irish prog rock movement. Fruupp commissioned a Fogel for the cover for their fifth album but the band split before it could be used. Jim Fitzpatrick was an avid fan, as was Steve Hillage whose interest continued into the rave era and who introduced Alex Paterson and Bill Drummond to her. Post-rockers God is an Astronaut followed Fogel keenly and a small press published a limited and expensive album of her images. Fogels sold to celebrity aficionados like Tilda Swinton and Nicolas Cage for high enough prices to sustain her and, when her skill and health began to ebb, arrange nursing care.

Ria had no opinions on Tilda Swinton, but she appreciated Nicolas Cage in an ironic way and was curious as to what he saw in these wall-filling canvases of purples, blacks, silver and diamonds.

'What is Bird Spirit Land?' Ria asked.

'The land beyond.' Ria curled Mrs Fogel's fingers round the ergonomic cutlery. She did not need to have her food cut up, but the time of feeding was surely coming. 'The repository of all souls. We come from it, we return to it, after a time we re-enter the world again. Oh, but it is full of chirps and twittering – they are always singing there. And wings! Birds are chaos. Look at the starlings! Chaos and life.'

Later, over bananas and carton custard, she looked up, eyes bright and said, 'Murmuration! Is there a finer word? A murmuration.'

That evening, as Ria walked up to the bus stop, she noticed the flock in the cold clear sky over the Waterworks: a moving cloud that changed direction, colour, shape, form in a moment. Living movement. She stopped, trying to predict its next shift, next wave or density. She could not. She watched so long she missed her bus and her 6.30 Zumba class at the leisure centre.

A murmuration. It must always have been there, hanging in the air. Every evening she had walked past, unseeing. What energy threw them into the sky, sent them storming and veering and flocking?

———

After the murmuration, the chimney breast looked bare and accusing. Every creak and click of the old gatehouse settling into another season seemed to emanate from the flue. Soot and old feathers stirring. Called to renewed motion. A bird is motion or it is nothing. The spirit needed placating. Settling, pinning down into death.

She picked one of the smaller, more easily transported paintings from a high, easily overlooked place above a door. It was still so cumbersome she had to wrap it in a sheet to hide her theft. It sat propped up in the wheelchair and baby-buggy space on the bus. She guarded it from the glares of the buggy-mothers, then humped the unwieldy thing down the road to her house through a steepening drizzle. It was slightly too wide for the chimney. Ria could live with that. It depicted a breaking wave of stars that flowed into birds, that swirled to become women fringed in rainbow. She could live with that too. She could live with it even better after she Googled Anna Fogel and saw the prices. Her spirit cage. Her hedge against unemployment.

———

The noise woke her, a scolding, chattering in the early light. A rattling, a racket of accusation and counter-accusation. She opened the curtains. On the flowerbed outside her gate at the road junction a gang of magpies stamped and stabbed and squawked. They stood in a ring around a solitary bird that fluttered and flapped and tried to escape. At every attempt it was brought down by beaks and feet.

'Leave it alone.' Ria shouted. She banged the window. The magpies looked up. Each fixed her an eye, then as one went back to their persecution. A beak stabbed, seized a tail feather, plucked it out. The victim turned to confront the attacker, another beak struck from the rear and stole a feather from a wing. The bird's rattling cries became shrieks of distress. Ria took a shoe, ran to the front door. 'Away, you dirty birds!'

She flung the shoe hard. The mob scattered up into the morning air. The victim hobbled away, bleeding, beating flightless wings. Tail, wing, breast feathers lay on bare soil where council gardeners had dug up summer flowers.

'Are you all right?' Ridiculous to ask, but she must ask. The maimed magpie hopped away from her, flapped up on to her recycle bin. Ria's thoughts of rescue, the vet up the road, rehabilitation evaporated at an alien eye, a sharp beak. This was not her business.

She had witnessed a judging and a punishment.

That evening she looked for the magpie in case it had died during the day, but magpies can only ever be found when you don't want them.

In the end Mrs Fogel failed.

The family descended even as Ria and Joanne were clearing, cleaning and packing the medical equipment. Dismal, disgusting work; wiping and coiling tubes, rolling sacs. Ria had never suspected family. Mrs Fogel had never spoken of family. Yet here they were, dark clothed, picking through rooms, poking at paintings, peering at the unfinished work in the studio. Ria understood why Mrs Fogel never spoke of them. They were vile. They resented Ria and Joanne's presence in the house. This stuff should have been cleared before their arrival. They had eyes only for market value. They knew nothing of Bird Spirit Land and the old lady's mythology. Learning Mrs Fogel, appreciating her skill and vision had been a work of years for Ria. These people clattered in in their hard shoes and dark suits and scattered everything. Valuers arrived; advised; allocated. By the time the van arrived to take the care equipment away, the house was stripped. Bird Spirit Land was dispersed.

'Wish I'd kept one of those weird paintings now,' Joanne said over the coffee you have when everything breaks and there is no clear course through the pieces to the future. 'They went for them first. Did you see?'

'Bird Spirit Land,' Ria said. 'She believed your soul flies through it from one life to the next.'

'Mad,' Joanne said. 'You got anything lined up?'

'I need time away. A career break.'

———————

Autumn darkened into winter and Ria's career break went from hiatus to sustained unemployment. Mrs Fogel's house had shown Ria the virtues of fastidious hoarding but even buffed by Universal Credit her savings were dwindling fast. She should move out of the lodge – she did not like the lodge, had never felt welcomed by the lodge – but she hated sharing space more than she hated the uncertainty of when the agency would call with new work.

She cut back on food, heating, clothes, memberships and lost short wet days tracking Fogel sales at online auctions. The reserves were impressive. The prices in the room were staggering. She tracked patterns of sales and resale, buyers and agents and mapped the big collectors and the celebrity buyers.

One Fogel to Nick Cage would set her up. For years. Timing was everything. And a good back story to the painting hanging on her chimney. Provenance. A gift from Mrs Fogel. For loyalty. She established places and times, asked for work references, polished her story so smooth and bright it blinded her. It was a gift: no doubt.

Now that she was minded to sell the painting she saw new things in it. The star swirls shone brighter. The rainbow fringes moved in the corner of her eye. She saw new faces in star fields, in feather patterns, in flowers and the whorled bark of the trees that were not quite trees.

Souls dwelt in Bird Spirit Land until the next life drew them on.

Souls sparkled on her chimney.

She found a dealer willing to come out to view the Fogel on the basis of her phone photographs. He made an appointment the following week. Ria approved. He was checking out her provenance. He came to the house on an evening of swirling rain; a neat man, too dapper for Belfast. Apart from questions on her provenance he had little chat and no banter.

Ria approved. He was double-checking her story.

He leaned close to the Fogel. Ria imagined the light of a thousand spirit-stars reflecting from his glasses.

'This is early,' he said. 'She was still evolving the mythos.'

'Is this good?' Ria asked.

'Early is good. I'd like to take some photographs.'

'Use mine,' Ria insisted.

He smiled and said he would be back with an offer. He phoned two days later. Ria would have got more selling direct to a buyer, but it was high for a dealer. He had an aficionado in the mood to spend money. Nicolas or Tilda? Or another, more mysterious collector? Elon? That vacuum cleaner guy?

'Let me think about it.'

'It won't go up.'

'I know.'

The offer wasn't generous but it was life-changing. Her own place. Her own time. A foot on a rung.

It would never do to be too eager, so she made the dealer wait. Two days.

'Cheque?' he said.

'Bank transfer.'

'Bank draft,' he said.

'Deal. Come over tonight.'

She hadn't gone past the house since Mrs Fogel died – it was not on any of her routes – but she needed to see it before the painting left. A closing. An approval. Absolution by bricks and mortar. She walked up Cavehill Road, past the Waterworks. Too early for starlings. A For Sale sign stood attached to the gate post. The house looked broken. From the road she could see through uncurtained windows into high empty rooms, bare floored, tide-marked where furniture stood for decades against wallpaper. There was nothing here to bless or damn. It was just property.

As she looked at the old house, the starlings rose behind her into the early twilight. Ria walked back down the road and they dashed and swooped, gathered and scattered above her. The murmuration was strong this evening: Ria was not the only one to stop and wonder at the patterns in the orange twilight. A sudden change of direction darkened half the sky with wings. A whipping tornado of birds rose and split into two elongated funnels, then merged over the upper reservoir. The bird-cloud rose like boiling smoke, towered over Ria. Flowed, and was a face.

The old woman's face. In the sky. All the sky. Looking at Ria. The lips parted. The mouth filled with dark, storming birds.

She ran. Ran into the side streets, away from the thing in the sky. Ran not looking back for fear it was following her. Ran across the road traffic hooting, braking, swerving. Did not stop running until her front door was locked behind her and the blinds pulled.

The painting blazed. Every star burned with the light of another world.

She hid in the kitchen. The house shivered with otherworldly energy. She texted the dealer. Pick it up right away.

After the painting was gone the house thrummed like a rung bell for hours. The envelope containing the bank draft lay on the kitchen table. Ria could not look at it. At last the echoes faded and the house was possessed by an enormous, beautiful silence. Ria cracked the living room door. Nothing. She opened it fully and stepped into the room. The air was cool, sweet, still, and Ria knew Mrs Fogel was gone.

A soul may become trapped in Bird Spirit Land if the doors from it are closed.

The scratch came from behind her head. Ria woke instantly, completely. She held her breath, waiting to be sure she had heard what she feared she'd heard. Again: this time a rattle. A weak flutter in the wall behind her headboard. Ria bolted from her bed, backed as far as she could from the wall. Another shake of feathers, louder, stronger: from the wall to her right. She jolted away as if electrocuted. Another scratch from beneath the floorboards. Now a rustle of many feathers from the ceiling. Her bedroom was a murmuration of beating wings.

Ria bolted, slammed the door, but the wings followed her along the hall: inside the walls, under the floor, in the roof spaces. She opened the living room door and a thunder like an entire flock taking flight hit her.

Now the tappings. Each louder, more insistent than the one before. Beaks, pecking at the masonry from the dark side. Pecking through to light and air.

The kitchen. Her sanctuary, her safe place. Ria slid the folding table against the door, pulled a chair to the centre of the floor. She sat hunched, a bread knife in her right fist. The cooing began. First in the wall with the living room, then inside the cupboards on that wall. The racket of magpies joined from floor and ceiling. New voices answered from the other walls: the hack of jackdaws, the accusation of rooks, shrieking seagulls. A cacophony of birds.

Ria looked up. She heard plaster crack and tumble in the hall.

They were coming.

She flung the knife with all her strength. It spun across the floor. In that moment of distraction she ran out the back door.

Into darkness.

The wing-storm enveloped her; a gyre of birds so dense it shut out the world. She struck at it; the murmuration flowed from her fist and reformed. She turned to run to the house. There was no path, no house, nothing but rushing, shrilling birds. She no longer knew where the house was. She no longer knew where she was. Then she did.

She beat, kicked out at the bird-storm but each time it flowed beyond her touch and regrouped. Each time closer. Ria gagged at the acid reek of bird feathers. The heat of their bodies was foul suffocation. A wing brushed her skin. Another, another. She was wrapped in a spinning shroud of smooth, warm, reeking feathers. She tried to beat the filthy wings away. She could not move her arm. Tried to run. Her legs were imprisoned. Tried to lunge but soft wings had turned to hard steel, closing around her. She yelled, she heaved, she could not move a finger.

A trapped soul may escape Bird Spirit Land if another takes its place.

Then Ria understood where she was, and how long she would stay here, and the screaming began. But what came from her lips, echoing up and down the endless black pipe, was the despairing shriek of a magpie.

Silent Valley

Sam Thompson

EOIN woke in the night, crying for his mother. She had been calling to him again. I held him close while he insisted that she was waiting and we must go. After he settled I lay listening to the silence of the small hours, to the scrabbling in the alley behind the house.

Just before dawn I lit the lamp, packed the rucksack with our last tins and filled the canteen at the water drum. Eoin said nothing when I told him we were leaving. His teeth chattered while I dressed him. Out in the morning dark he would not let go of my hand.

We walked from Stranmillis to the Ormeau Bridge without meeting a soul. The bonfires smouldered on the Embankment, silhouetting the charred bodies of witches on the scaffold poles. Witchfinding was on the rise again and every night new towers of pallets, furniture and tyres burned for the punishment of those found guilty of trafficking with forbidden powers.

These days I avoided our few remaining neighbours. The last time we went to market, as I was bartering paracetamol for an old woman's jar of peanut butter, Eoin had announced without warning that his mother was waiting for him in the Silent Valley. I hushed him, but the woman stared and made a sign to ward off the evil eye.

———————

Grey dawn on the Ormeau Road. We picked through the gridlock, the cars, vans and buses resting on their axles, their windscreens blind with lichen. To our left, beyond the Ravenhill, lay the plantation zone that had swallowed most of east Belfast. It pressed on my awareness like a headache, but I did not look.

The plantations had appeared six years ago, soon after Eoin's third birthday. They came all at once, seeming to unfold from a hidden dimension. Some engulfed whole districts while others occupied a few streets or even single buildings. It was impossible to say more about them because they were immune to human perception. Once or twice in those early days I strayed too close to an interface and ended up with a blank in my memory: a region of magnetised dread that repelled any attempt at scrutiny.

Within a week of the incursion more than half our neighbours had gone missing, taken away, and a language of euphemisms sprung up among the survivors. We spoke of *the other fellers* and *the kindly folk* if we had to speak of such things at all. We had our rituals of propitiation. No one was foolish enough to handle money now or use an electrical device, and every house had symbols carved on the doors and bits of iron nailed to the lintels. Gangs broke the legs of those suspected of carelessness. Over time the disappearances slowed, but a year later we were the only family still living on Stranmillis Park. Sometimes I thought we must have an unsuspected talent for denial, for not seeing and not speaking. Perhaps, I thought, it was this that had kept us safe.

Eoin clung to my hand and walked in dogged silence. Half an hour brought us to the ruins of Forestside, where we found that local militia had barricaded the main road with shopping trolleys. They waved us forward and it was too late not to obey. There were seven of them, none older than twenty, shorn-headed, armed with hatchets and crowbars. They looked askance at Eoin, wondering why a boy tall enough to recruit was hiding against his father like a child. They questioned us about our journey, but all they really wanted was the rucksack. A toll for our passage, they said.

In any case we could not go back. They ushered us through the roadblock and watched until we were out of sight. We continued south, past rows of abandoned vehicles as mossy as burial mounds.

It took us five hours to walk into an ambush.

The carriageway had brought us under banks of forest and between crumpled hills. The light drained since daybreak from the overcast sky. We passed farmhouses and old manses defeated long ago by the weather, roofs fallen in. More than once I was sure of being watched from the windows.

Eoin trudged beside me without complaint. His lips were blue but when I asked if he was cold he said he did not know. He did not know if he was hungry either. Once he tripped and fell but he made no sound as I helped him up. I told him to clap his hands and stamp his feet, though when I did the same it was no help to my numb extremities.

We paused near a dead petrol station on the approach to Ballynahinch. This was the first real town we had encountered. There was no telling whether it was deserted or who or what its inhabitants might be. I told Eoin we would find something to eat in there and some way to get warm. We passed the Annunciation Grammar School, a hulk of scorched steel and concrete that had once been a glassy modern building. Here, under the supervision of the nuns, Saoirse had shed her last scraps of childhood Catholicism and aced her A-levels before leaving for university in London. We met there as students, moved in together soon after graduating and were staunch Londoners for a decade. It was only when we decided to have a baby that Saoirse changed her mind. In spite of her contempt for those nuns, she discovered that she could not imagine bringing up a child anywhere except her own part of the world.

When I told English friends and colleagues that we were relocating, most were baffled. Moving to Belfast, they said: that's not something you hear very often. They asked cautiously if I wasn't concerned about the politics and the economy over there, or about whether I would be welcome. When I mentioned the plans to our next-door neighbour, a solicitor in his sixties, he shook his head and told me I was making a mistake. They're friendly on the surface, he said, but underneath there's something nasty. You'll see.

Saoirse was pregnant with Eoin by the time we moved. I felt we were starting a new life. We had found a nice little terraced house on Stranmillis Park and I was glad to be free of London – of the commute and the expense, and of the delusion, as I now saw it, of being at the centre of the world. If I sometimes felt like an outsider, the compensation was seeing Saoirse flourish. It was not only the pregnancy. She liked talking to people on the street here, joking and laughing more than she ever had in England, using turns of phrase I had never heard from her before. All of a sudden she was involved in campaigns about secular education and cross-community government. She took the new baby on marches for reproductive rights and equal marriage. I realised she had been waiting for years to play her part in these fights. If I found myself a little homesick, I realised, it was my turn; besides,

I was beginning to feel involved. While Saoirse fed a seven-month-old Eoin I scowled at the TV news, at an English politician standing in Westminster and calmly explaining that in relations with Europe the principle of national sovereignty was paramount. Does he actually not get the irony here, I asked. And does he not realise that thanks to him my son is now significantly more likely to get blown to bits by dissident paramilitaries? What?

She was smiling.

Now you're a proper Norn Iron dad.

That time came back to me as we stole through Ballynahinch. We worked our way along the High Street, watching for signs of life, keeping in the shelter of the gutted shops. Eoin's fingers were limp and solid as if chilled through the marrow. I was kneeling in front of him, blowing on his fingertips in my cupped hands, when somebody chuckled behind me.

We were surrounded by a group of men in balaclava helmets. They carried an assortment of objects: billhooks, shovels, buckets, lengths of chain. In spite of the cold, all of them were naked from neck to waist, and each had the same pattern of scars across his chest: a word in unknown characters, carved into each man's bluish flesh. Before I could tell Eoin to run they broke my nose, grabbed him and dragged us into the town.

On the day Saoirse went missing, we had an argument – or rather we had been bickering all day, unable to settle on what we really wanted to fight about. I was in a bad mood, feeling sorry for myself, brooding about what might be happening in England. Communication at a distance being over, I had no way to find out what had become of my parents in Hertfordshire or my siblings in London and Hull.

Saoirse was trying to get Eoin to read to her. We were concerned about how long it was taking him to get the hang of books. These things still mattered, we told one another – now more than ever – but we could not make him cooperate. He acted much younger than his age. Sometimes I imagined that when the plantations arrived something inside him had changed too: something had got stuck, some line of development pushed off course. I could hear Saoirse's patience shortening and Eoin edging closer to a tantrum. He was rocking and whingeing, trying to wriggle away from her and complaining that he was too tired.

I was tired myself, my head aching and my guts hollow. When Eoin finally tipped from sulky resistance into a meltdown, bawling at the top of his lungs and battering his heels on the floor, I gave Saoirse a look to say she should have known better. She glared back. The arguments did not have to be restated. She had to push him because I did not bother. It was my fault that she was to blame. She pressed her fists to her temples and went into the bedroom, while I began to lecture Eoin about how it was time to grow up. He could not hear me, but I went on, as though I could prove Saoirse wrong by scolding him enough. He lay on his side, his face to the wall, growling and shrieking to shut me out. In the end I threw up my hands, got my kit together and headed out on a scavenging run.

Two hours later I turned back on to Stranmillis Park. I had been over to the Lisburn Road, searching for likely pickings among the grand houses hidden away in those quiet streets, finding nothing. Then I had noticed the light was fading and all at once I could not understand why I had stayed away so long. How could I have left them without making things right between us? Once we were together we would be ourselves again, I told myself, and hiked home as fast as I could.

Eoin and Saoirse were out in the street. Both were motionless, as if fixed in place. Eoin stood in front of the house and gazed at his mother. Her back was turned to him, her arms raised in what might have been a gesture of protection or warning, or a kind of salute, and her face was lifted towards … what?

I saw it, I was certain of that, but afterwards I could not tell what I had seen. I could only sift through broken images: a form like an oak tree, a crown of flowers that were not flowers, a gigantic orangutan shaggy with moss, an empty suit of medieval plate armour that had been left to corrode on the ocean bed until its surface rotted to brittle green lacework and bright corals spilled out at the joints. These fragments did not piece together.

The visitor towered over Saoirse and she walked towards it. I must have called out, because she looked at me. Her eyes were bright as it lifted her off her feet, pale green brambles curling around her waist. After that, all I remembered was the crackling of wet twigs as the thing unlimbered itself, the single uncanny movement in which it rushed towards me and was gone, and Eoin's solemn eyes as I faced him along the empty street.

———————

We walked hand in hand on rising ground. The mountains were close, the foothills nosing in, and the road offered us to all the scrutiny the sky might hold. I felt we had been walking for many hours, many more than a day could contain, but I did not remember sleeping or stopping to eat. My sinuses tasted rusty and my cheekbones were still ringing with pain, but I could not recover the sequence of events. I had images of blunt hands thrusting us down a passageway of corrugated iron, and of Eoin falling into a yard with his wrists bound. A ladderback chair stood on tarmac blanched with frost. In memory, Eoin's terror was a substance, thickening the air and spreading from him in waves that ran off into the derelict streets of the town: there they did not vanish but swirled and mounted into a rustling, giggling noise that swelled all around us, making the men pause and look about. I remembered Eoin telling me to keep my eyes closed until it was over, and then the screaming and the beating of wings.

And now I found us walking. Eoin was setting our pace, leading me without hesitation as if the map in him was growing clearer. We had come to the mountains from behind, I felt: these were not the soft blue shapes that had hovered above seaside towns on weekend outings in the old life, but a landscape of steep access roads, hidden reservoirs, barren slopes, old engineering. It was not a landscape made for us.

The light had almost gone when we topped a rise and saw the house. It was long and sprawling, perhaps a kind of gatehouse, set behind a stone wall and a big iron gate with paint coming away in shards of pillar-box red. Unlike the other houses we had seen on our journey, it was not a ruin. The tiles were intact and the windows unbroken. Eoin tried to drag me past, up the track towards the darkening trees. We had to keep moving, he told me, we were almost there – but I made him stop. I strained my eyes into the house's gloom, almost sure that I had seen a flicker behind the glass. I was treading towards the front door when it opened and a woman stepped out. When she saw us she showed no surprise. Her hair had grown long. Her breath made a plume in the dimming air, and in the swaying light of a candle her face was strange as only the most familiar faces can be.

———

She stirred up the fire, let us peel off our sodden clothes and gave us blankets. She gave us potato soup and nettle tea and we ate sitting cross-legged on the hearth. The parlour was lit only by firelight and the sky outside the window was a ribbon of pale gold fading behind the trees. She stood by the mantel but did not try to come near. She watched Eoin until he grew shy and burrowed his head under my arm. A minute later he was asleep. She studied his face.

She did not know what her name was. She did not know how she had come to be living in this house, or how long she had been here, or how she had survived. She could not remember any time before this: it was as if she had sprung into existence yesterday, or at the moment we had come in sight of the house. When I asked if she knew us, her brow creased in the way it always did when she could not make up her mind.

Reunions were a puzzle, I thought, only half-awake. To meet the person you know best in the world after a long absence and in an unexpected place: how will you recognise one another, and how will you be sure? I almost had the answer, but as she settled by the hearth to watch over us I felt the difficulty was too great.

When she woke me the fire had died and starlight grinned through the glass. She was grasping for my hands like someone suffering night terrors.

Is it you, she was asking. Is it you?

Yes, I told her, it's me, it's us.

I don't know where I am, she said. I think I'm not here.

She was shivering wildly, and all I could think to do was hold open the heap of blankets so that she could curl herself in beside Eoin. We lay on the hearth, holding one another, unable to find words of comfort, until we slept.

———————

So we have come to the Silent Valley.

This morning I woke in daylight to Eoin shaking my shoulder, and sat up, bone-chilled and disoriented, brushing away the dead leaves that lay on me like a blanket, to find that we had been sleeping in the open. I looked around, confounded. The house of last night had dissolved and we had woken up in the archaeology of a house, broken down and roofless, given over to the weather. Crumbled ridges marked where walls had once been, and a stub of chimney stood like an ivy-wrapped memorial stone. Leaves lay heaped in the corners, glistening with frost.

We have walked up the short track from the house through the trees and the abandoned car park. Once this was a place for day trips, for families and new couples and ramblers wanting an easy walk. The remains are here – the lavatory block, the playground, the duck pond, the café with its picnic tables – but, like all traces of the old life, they have forgotten themselves. I have to stare a long time before I begin to remember what they are for.

Eoin leads me on, up the track, past other structures whose purposes are even more obscure: sunken blockhouses and great stone cubes that have no entrances I can see. The mountains surround us now, their high backs mottled with heather. An artificial chasm has been dug in the earth, a channel walled with huge stone blocks where a river flows over pavement far below.

We climb a broad, smooth slope, as steep and regular as the flank of a pyramid, and when we reach the top the landscape reveals itself. The glacial valley opens, granite domes receding into haze, countless mountainsides stepping in behind to deepen the perspective. It folds around us. The reservoir is brimming, the vast dark body of the water barely ruffled by the wind, reaching far between the mountains and out of sight. The spillway shaft is a funnel plunging into the dark. The water bursts into whiteness as it cascades down the ancient brickwork and I can hear the roar.

We are climbing the first mountainside, wading through heather and gorse. We look down on the reservoir and it is already small enough to cover with my hand. These mountains that were a prospect in the distance are now the ground under my feet. I cannot find the moment at which the one becomes the other, but it keeps happening as we push on along the valley. My knees ache and I think Eoin must tire soon, but he is pulling ahead, gaining vigour as we go. When I pause to get my breath he does not stop and I hasten not to be left behind.

Often I think we are coming to a crest or a summit – a place where we can rest and see the whole landscape spread below – but when we get there, another prospect opens and we have to keep climbing. Perspective shifts and the distance withdraws. Eoin walks on and when I ask where he is heading he does not hear.

The question has no answer. I am not to ask where we have come from, or where she is to be found. Eoin strides into the mountains, fast and strong, and my task is to follow him. Now that we are here we will always be here. We are always going further in. We walk, and we will walk, until all we are is walking.

The Tempering

Michelle Gallen

A S a child I loved my father more fiercely than any lioness has ever loved her first-born male cub. If he'd let me, I would've licked him with a tongue as rough as sandpaper until he bled. I would've swallowed him whole and kept him safe in my belly, like that wolf who devoured a grandmother and cradled her snoring in his guts, until they were both rudely awakened by the woodcutter's axe.

But my kind father fell ill one wintery evening. Though he was a man who did not easily take to his bed, he went upstairs dark-faced, clutching his head, and did not come back down. My mother called the doctor who spoke of an ambulance, which my father refused.

One night I was wakened by knocking at the door. I slipped to the window and saw the priest's car outside. The bald moon stared at me hungrily as I listened to the murmur of my mother's prayers and the grumble of the priest performing the Last Rites. My mother told us the next morning that the sacrament had worked, but it was weeks before my father came back downstairs, to sit in his armchair by the fire, where he drank strong tea. I kept an eye on this thin man, who seemed to have swallowed moonlight, who did not smile when we sang, who pushed me from his knee when I climbed up for a hug.

This moon father grew angrier as he grew stronger, stamping around like an ogre in a castle, smashing plates, thumping on doors, breaking hearts that shattered so quietly I like to believe he never heard. I tried for a long time not to hate him. I tried not to hate him when he taught us one lesson after another, like how we must wear woollen tights to hide the bruises he had made bloom on our legs. If we let our bruises be seen, he warned, the busybodies in the social workers' office would swarm into our house and carry us off, leaving him and mother alone by the fire. He noted that the hiding of bruises was in our interest, not his, for he and mother would be perfectly happy to sit by the fire, drinking cups of Ovaltine, listening to the radio with the moon spilling over the floor.

I tried not to hate him when he said he'd shoot the dog if none of us would drown her litter. Instead I volunteered to drown the pups. As a reward, my father allowed me to pick which dog would be allowed to live. I pointed at the ugliest pup, the runt that I often found lying cold and senseless on the coal shed floor having been shoved off the blanket by its stronger brothers. I'd revived the runt time and again by tucking it inside my jumper to warm it up against my own useless nipples, before pushing it on to its mother's teats to suck. My father put the runt to the side, then dropped the other pups into a sack. He handed it to me with orders to head for the stream in our neighbour's field.

I tried not to hate him though February sliced through me like a knife as I stood by the stream wondering how to drown the pups. Drowning seemed all too easy on TV. The public information films broadcast every summer warned us that walks by the river could easily result in the sodden corpse of a small child. My mother told stories of weans taken by waves as they played on the beach, their crab-infested bodies found days or weeks later. In books and movies, the battle against drowning involved lifeguards and flotation devices, rescue boats and lifebuoys, mermaids and prayers. I didn't know if pups could swim or float, but my natural caution kept me from casting one into the stream to check: I didn't want to risk the sight of a pup paddling downstream. I had learned from comics that baddies sometimes dumped unwanted kittens into weighted sacks before throwing them in the river. Goodies would then put themselves in peril to rescue the animals, taking them home, drying them off, feeding them saucers of cream (in our house, it was my father who supped the creamy top from each pint of milk, leaving us the blueish-grey dregs for our cornflakes).

I emptied the sack, weighted it with stones, then placed

the pups on top. I tied the mouth of the sack, then threw it into the stream. I soon learned that the stream was too shallow for the sack to submerge and that week-old pups can doggy paddle. I waited, hoping that the pups would grow tired and go under. But I grew weary before they did, and pulled the sack back to me. After some consideration, I resolved to drown the puppies by hand. The first pup was the hardest, for I made the mistake of looking into its just-opening eyes. They were filmy and unfocussed and though I suspected it was blind, I felt something pierce me before I plunged it into the water. I held it down until it stopped paddling, which happened long after my hand went numb. I anchored it under a stone in a calm pool before selecting the next pup. This one I squeezed sharply before holding it in the water. My instincts were good: with less air in its lungs, it drowned faster. When all five pups lay under stones, I heard a huff of breath from behind. I turned and saw several young bull calves pawing the ground and tossing their heads. They were in a mood familiar to me, torn between playfulness and murder. I considered abandoning the bodies, but recalled my father saying it wasn't nice to leave dead animals in a stream where they'd pollute the water. It was better, he had said – far better – to leave them in a ditch so they'd be eaten instead of going to waste. I kept my eyes on the young bulls as I transferred the dead puppies into the sack. Then I waded through the water to the barbed wire on the other side of the stream and threw the sack over.

I slipped between the wires, slung the sack over my shoulder and set off towards the bristle of whin bushes at the far end of the field. Halfway there I heard a sigh from behind me. I whipped around, ready for a bull calf or a bad-tempered ram, but saw nothing. I walked on. Then I heard a whimper from inside the sack. I kept walking. By the time I reached the ditch, the puppies were squirming against my back. I had not done a good job. I hated myself at that moment, standing soaked to the arse and elbow, my face wet with tears. I hated myself, and I hated him.

After I handed my father the empty sack (which we reused, time and again, in the years that followed) I went to my mother who clucked and fussed over me, rubbed my hands between hers to warm them. We watched my father go past the window with a chainsaw slung on his shoulder. I asked my mother what she thought would happen if my father died. She told me not to worry and explained that if he died of sickness or by accident, or was murdered in his bed, we'd be awarded enough money to pay off our mortgage and leave us with, if not riches, *enough*. As the chainsaw began to spit and snarl up the yard I pictured the calm that would descend on our mortgage-free home, imagined the Ovaltine I'd sip with my mother by the fire, and considered how I would go about killing him.

Late that spring, I watched him pump weedkiller on to the wild verges where we harvested seeds and berries for magic potions. Even his gas mask wore a look of pitiless focus; he missed not one blade of grass, not one blossom. The butterflies that lit on the sprayed flowers flew drunkenly afterwards, then fell to the tarmac, flapping sporadically, until our cat – who had a long history of trying and failing to catch butterflies – licked them up. I spent some time considering how many poisoned butterflies it might take to kill or at least incapacitate the cat, but the conundrum made my brain hurt: it was the sort of problem I was not very good at solving in maths class. I retreated indoors to where my mother was feeding the latest baby (I'd come to understand that there would always be more babies, who would arrive – if not quite as predictably as Easter or Christmas – at least as regularly). I was peeling spuds when there was a knock at the door. My mother sent me to answer while she covered herself up. Two pale men stood on the doorstep. They were perturbed to see me standing in their way.

'Where's your mammy?' one asked, exchanging what I knew was a significant look with the other.

'She's inside, minding the baby,' I said, playing for time. My mother had taught me that feeding babies with what she called her bosoms (but most local men called her diddies) was natural and normal. Yet her reaction to our male neighbours 'dropping in' without knocking suggested there was also something if not sacred, then at least private, about the process.

'We need to come in to see your mammy,' said the taller man, stepping forward. I didn't move. I wasn't scared he'd punch me. He seemed like a dam, brimming with water, in danger of overflowing at any minute.

'Mammy,' I shouted, 'There's two men here to see you.'

'Coming in a minute,' she shouted back.

I stood before the men thinking of the way I pegged my father's pants on the line to dry in the wind. They'd come to his drawer smelling sometimes of spring, sometimes of sun, but more often of slurry.

'Grand weather we're having,' I said to the men who exchanged a frown before replying.

'Great altogether,' the smaller one said.

I had to drape my mother's damp pants in the hot press, where they dried in the dark, becoming infused with the smell of mouse droppings (though when she dropped her used pants into the laundry basket, they smelt strongly – lustily – of between her legs).

———————

'Bridie, Bridie, we're awful sorry for your trouble,' said the smaller man, grabbing my mother's right hand between his own meaty paws. My mother looked at the men, then down at me in confusion. The taller man had pursed his lips and was staring at my mother's feet as though she was wearing the saddest slippers he had ever seen.

'Where's Paddy?' the smaller man said.

'Paddy? He's in the garden,' my mother said with relief. 'You can head out back to see him.'

The two men glanced at each other.

'He's in the garden?' the taller one said and my mother nodded and half-turned to bring them through the house. But the smaller man still had her hand. He held her in the doorway.

'He's in the garden. I'll take ye to him,' she said encouragingly, pulling her hand away and retreating into the house. They came in after her. The taller man guided her towards the chair that was still warm from her buttocks and pushed her into it. She plopped down with a look of surprise. She was not frightened of these men, not yet.

'You stay here now, Bridie, and rest yourself. Don't you worry your head any more,' the taller one said. The smaller man – with the look of a terrier sniffing out a rat – ducked into the living room and sitting room before checking the bedrooms. He came back into the kitchen, frowning.

'Nothing,' he said, 'I can't find him.'

'He's in the garden I'm telling you,' my mother said, a little frustrated now. 'I'll take you to him.' She tried to rise, but the larger man dropped a heavy hand on her shoulder.

'Ah now, no no no no. You sit where you are, Bridie. Go easy now,' he said to her.

'Go ring Doctor O'Neill,' he said to the other man.

My mother glared at me. 'Get you outside now and bring

your father in,' she ordered. Before the smaller man could grab me, I darted out the back door and ran to my father. He stood in a haze of poison, haloed by dying butterflies. I shouted over that two men were there to see him. He noted my agitation, pulled off his mask and stared at me with hard eyes.

'What sort of men?' he asked.

'A big one and a wee-er one,' I answered.

'Uniforms?' I shook my head.

'Balaclavas?' Again, I shook my head. He laid his pump and mask on the ground and tramped over the butterflies towards the house. I skipped around the cat, which was staggering on the drive, and entered the house on my father's heels. The smaller man went grey as a ghost when he caught sight of my father.

'Paddy,' he said, dropping the phone.

'Brendan,' my father answered as the phone clattered off the floor and bounced up and down on the coiled wire. He strode into the kitchen where the other fellow was guarding my mother. 'Mick,' he said.

The tall man spun around and stared open-mouthed at my father. 'Paddy?'

'I told you he was in the garden,' my mother said, crossly. She got to her feet and went to fill the kettle. I loitered nearby until I understood what had happened. It transpired that a man with the same name as my father, of a similar age, who was also known for his skill at football, had dropped dead that morning. After word had gone out about this death, someone had confused my living father with the deceased man. Mick and Brendan had tidied themselves up and rushed to our house to offer their condolences. When my mother had said my father was in the garden, they were sure she'd cracked and thought she'd have to be put away. Mick admitted that when he couldn't find my father laid out in the house, he'd half-feared my mother – in her fit of madness – had buried him in the garden. They had a great laugh at the misunderstanding, then my father rang the priest and local newsagent to put an end to the rumour.

'I'm not dead at all,' I heard my father say down the phone, 'It was all a misunderstanding.'

I went back into the garden and stood among the wilting flowers, watching the cat vomit butterfly wings on to the drive. I knew without a flicker of doubt that my kind and lovely father – the one from my early childhood – was dead and had been for a long time. I realised that he'd been stolen from me The Night of the Last Rites, swapped with this dead-eyed creature who had a moon for a heart. I vowed to hunt down my real father's body so I could unmask this ghoul, leaving my family free to mourn and eligible for the life insurance money.

I took the initiative, organising my brothers and sisters into a team. We started digging in the garden, careful to avoid the cat's grave. When adults asked what we were at, I told them we were digging for gold (which stretched the truth, but was far from a lie). My siblings were often distracted by the things we found – shards of broken china, worms, rusty nails, beetles – but week by week, bone by bone, we began to amass a skeleton in our Secret Den. When the dog dragged a sheep's head into our yard, we watched her lap the festering brains from the skull before crowning our bone pile with it in lieu of our father's head. We continued our search for a human skull, shining a torch down the old well behind the house, poking sticks into ditches, dredging pond sludge with old pairs of my mother's tights, catching tiny freshwater shrimps that flicked and twitched in the palm of my hand for longer than you'd think before they died.

While we worked, our changeling father continued to stamp around the house, pouring petrol into ant nests, feeding jackdaws poisoned bread, whacking rabbits blinded by myxomatosis with a plank of wood, walloping us – randomly it seemed – with a hand as cold and hard as a shovel. But none of this mattered to me now: I knew it was only a matter of time before we proved that this creature was an imposter, before we exchanged our dead father's bones for gold.

But when winter came the ground froze and we could no longer dig. My siblings retreated indoors to the heat of the fire, leaving me to pace the frosty grass with my eyes closed, trying to sense where my father's skull lay.

The day the men in the red car came I was home alone, off school with a flu. They knocked at the door and when

I answered they barged in. One man pinned me to the floor, while the other checked each room, calling for my father.

'Where is he? Where the fuck is he?' the man on top of me shouted, though there was in truth no need to shout when he was that close to my ear. Realising who these men in balaclavas were, I answered truthfully.

'He's away to the shops with Mammy. He said he wouldn't be long.'

The man got up, pulled me to my feet and dragged me into the living room where he pushed me into my mother's chair. He paced the floor until the other man, the one calm and sure as the eye of a storm, came in and sat in my father's chair.

'So your daddy's at the shops, is he?'

I nodded, bright-eyed with fever.

'Grand. We're just going to wait here for him. We're friends of your daddy. We just need to have a wee chat with him.'

I eyed the gun in his hands. 'Are you not here to shoot him?'

Lightning flashed as he looked at me. I felt thunder rumble the ground between us.

'Aye. We are right enough,' he said with amusement. 'We're here to shoot him all right.'

He sat back in the chair and glanced up at the nervous man, who was fiddling with his gun.

'Put that away and go out and put on the kettle will ye,' he ordered, then looked back at me.

'Tay?'

I nodded, then chanced my arm. 'And a biccie?'

He nodded.

I detected a weakness. 'A chocolate biccie?'

He narrowed his eyes, then answered with a smile in his voice. 'Ach, go on then.'

We sat in companionable silence, listening to the kettle boil, the rattle of the other fella out in the kitchen as he tried to find cups, the splash of hot water as he scalded the heel of the pot, the clink of sugar before the splash of milk. He came back in to us clutching three mugs of tea.

'Where are the biccies?' he growled at me.

'Top cupboard,' I answered, understanding that this man did not have children.

I drank my tea the way he handed it to me, sweet, milky and blood hot. I ate my chocolate biccie, then asked for another one.

'You're some pup,' the calm man said approvingly, before passing me the biccie tin. It was clear these men were the answer to my problem.

'I need the toilet,' I said to the calm man.

'Go on then,' he said.

I slipped out of the room and ran up the stairs into my parents' bedroom and dialled 999. Shortly after I came back down, the phone rang. The two men looked at each other, then at me.

'Answer it,' the calm man said.

I picked up the receiver and listened. Then I held out the phone and said, 'There's a woman that wants to speak with Barry.'

The calm man, who did not look like a Barry to me, took it. I listened to his voice tighten as he spoke in the spaces where the woman's voice fell quiet.

'Right. Right you are. Right,' he said, though his tone gave me the impression things were far from right. He clattered the receiver down into the cradle and spoke over my head to the nervy man.

'He's been lifted. The Brits got him at a checkpoint out the Donegal road.'

'We'd better get the fuck out of here,' the other man said, glancing out the window. The calm man turned to me suddenly. I had the impression that he was smiling at me from underneath the balaclava, like when he'd allowed me the second biccie.

'Sweetheart, will you tell your daddy something for me?'

I nodded.

'You tell your daddy he's a dead man walking.'

'He's a dead man walking,' I repeated, to demonstrate my understanding. We stood there for a few seconds, eyeing each other.

After they drove off, I sat in my father's chair with the tin on my lap. I picked up a biccie, tore off the foil and bit into it.

I ate every single one, then sat rustling the golden wrappers in my hands. A long time later, when I heard the sound of our car in the yard, I stood up and threw the wrappers on to the dying fire. The gold burst into green-blue flames that danced briefly – gorgeously – on top of the smouldering embers.

Now and Then Some Washes Up

Carlo Gébler

PETER sat in the kitchen. It was August and he was alone. His parents, both teachers, had gone to their schools to prepare for the start of term. He heard the letter box snap. He hurried up the hall and saw a buff envelope on the mat. From the colour he knew his results had come.

Peter rang the history department at Queen's at nine.

'A and two Bs,' he told the secretary.

As he would be coming in September, they discussed accommodation.

'It's limited, even for first years,' she said. 'Find some digs.'

He went and bought a *Belfast Telegraph*. He found an ad for a room in Pretoria Street. He rang the phone number and arranged a viewing.

The next day he got the bus from Dungannon to Glengall Street and set out to cross the city on foot. All the pavements and the roads shimmered like water, he noticed. It was the glass from the windows of all the bombed buildings. On the journey he was searched four times. All the soldiers, he noticed, reeked of cordite.

He reached Pretoria Street and rang the bell. The landlady was stout and smelt of Germolene. She led him to the room. It was at the rear, north-facing, dark. There were dresses on the back of the door.

'Olivia's,' she explained. 'The lodger. She's going to Leeds. She's quite right. I'd leave myself if I could.'

Peter went to the window and looked down on a vast hydrangea bush, its blooms blue and stirring.

'My late husband kept a beautiful garden,' she said.

Unable to think of anything else to say he said, 'I'll take the room.'

'Deposit is two weeks' rent.'

He produced the signed Bank of Ireland cheque his mother had given him.

'Make it out to Mrs E.F. Smyth, Y not I,' she said.

He filled it in and handed it to her.

'You can move in the first of September,' said Mrs Smyth. 'Rent is always paid a week in advance.'

Later, Peter would look back on September 1st as the day he started his life, seeing as it was both his eighteenth birthday and the day he left home.

————————

Mrs Smyth served Peter his meals in the front room. It smelt of old apples.

One November night, gloomily spooning heavy oxtail soup into his mouth, Peter ran his eyes over the crowded shelves in the alcove by the fireplace. There was a World War I German bayonet, cut-glass decanters, a collection of porcelain shepherdesses – and what was this? It couldn't be.

He got up and went over. As he'd thought – it was a funerary urn for ashes with a plaque which he read: *Cecil Arbuthnot Horatio Smyth, 1888–1952.*

At that moment Mrs Smyth came in.

'You found him,' she said.

He turned. She had his main course: fish pie.

'I couldn't be separated,' she said, nodding at the urn. 'And with him up there, we can talk any time I need.'

She put down the fish pie, then went to adjust the curtains. They were yellow, heavy and smelt of coal smoke.

'I've actually got some of his ashes,' she said as she fiddled, 'in one of his old wage packets. I keep it in my handbag. When I get down, I dig it out and give it a squeeze. I always feel better then.'

She turned. Peter was standing very still, listening.

'Cecil's actually in the kitchen now. But when I go back down he'll slip upstairs to the landing. He's always nearby somewhere, only I never see him. I just hear him.'

———

Near Christmas Mrs Smyth showed him the wage packet with her husband's ashes.

'Go on,' she said to Peter, 'squeeze it.'

He did. The granules reminded him first of salt, and then of the ground glass that glistened in the streets when the moon shone.

In the New Year the papers were full of terrible statistics about 1972, the year just ended. Peter spent a lot of time wondering if he'd made a mistake staying. He could have gone to Manchester. After all, they'd asked for the same grades. He made enquiries. Yes, he could transfer, he gathered, but in the end he decided against: in England he'd be too far away if anything happened to his parents. So he stayed in Belfast, got his degree, and secured a place to do a DipEd. Like his parents, he'd be a teacher.

In the summer of 1976, before starting at Stranmillis, he left Mrs Smyth's and took a flat in Camden Street, sharing with two girls. One boiling summer's evening, when he came in, he found a rat in the Belfast sink in their kitchen.

He was carrying a long shallow wooden box which had originally been for oranges and which the greengrocer had given him to carry home his vegetables. Without thinking he dropped the box on to the rat and began to push it down. He heard the rat squealing and saw its thick, serrated tail thrashing as it struggled to get free. He kept pressing until he could hear and feel nothing. Then he piled tins and saucepans on top of the vegetables, dropped the plug into the plug hole, and turned on the cold water tap. He got the sink half full, but the weight of the tins and the saucepans was so great the box didn't float.

Come evening, he emptied everything and there it was, in the water, bloated, terrifying, its big white teeth showing. With the fire tongs he lifted the rat's corpse into the empty ash pail and then immediately closed the lid.

He picked up the pail and left the kitchen. His two flatmates were on the landing outside, their faces stricken.

'Oh my God!' said one. This was Mary. She was training to be a primary school teacher.

He tipped the rat into a bin in the entry and returned. He found Mary in the kitchen, drying the vegetables with a tea towel. Mary was from the Glens. She was small. She wore her hair in a bob.

'That was awful,' she said. 'But you were marvellous, a life-saver.'

She kissed him fiercely on the mouth.

———

Peter finished his DipEd and got a job in a grammar school in east Belfast. He married Mary. They bought a semi near the newly opened Mary Peters Track. They had a son, Paul. Peter made head of department by the time he was forty.

Then Peter's parents died and Mary's parents died and Paul left home and married and got a job in IT and Mary finally took early retirement. For years then she made theatre costumes: she also did make-up and stage management. Once, when drunk, she said to Peter, 'When you made head of department, why didn't you make me quit teaching straightaway? I hated it yet you made me do ten years more than I needed.' The next morning she denied saying what she said. But she had.

Peter retired at the start of the year he turned sixty-five. The question now was where they would live. They'd always thought they'd like to live by the sea but they couldn't afford Bangor or the north coast. They looked in Donegal but worried about what would happen if they got ill and needed the NHS. Then Mary spotted a house in Fermanagh with, according to the ad, 'Lakeside views and access'.

One spring morning they went down to see the property. It was a mock-Georgian new-build with a fanlight and wooden windows. The building stood on the summit of small hill reached by a steep asphalt drive and it overlooked Lough Coin.

The agent met them at the front door and brought them through the echoing square rooms that smelt of concrete and paint and then he led them down the driveway and across the road to a stretch of hard earth, enough for two cars to park on. There was a gap in the trees here and, on the other side, a hidden sandy beach with a rotted boat, its fallen timbers like a ribcage.

Ahead of them stretched the lake, silver and lustrous, dotted with swans, ducks and other birds. On the far side there was a fence running along the whole shoreline and behind this were fields filled with tiny cattle and still tinier sheep, and faraway an old farmhouse and some sheds. And that was it. There was nothing else.

'You get half the lake,' said the agent, 'plus the shore back to the road, which isn't much. And by the way, you'll never get planning permission to build on it, so don't even go there.'

'We won't be building,' said Mary. 'It's water we want.'

While she was speaking, Peter remembered Mr Smyth's ashes in his wage packet and the gritty feel when he squeezed. Of all the things he might recall, why, at this moment, was he remembering that? He couldn't fathom it.

'Peter,' he heard Mary say. 'Are you all right?'

'Sorry,' he said, and the memory vanished. 'I was miles away.'

'I thought you were having a turn,' she said.

On the way home, Mary said the house was their destiny and so they sold their semi and bought it and moved down. It all happened very quickly.

————————

A July evening, heavy and still and bright. Peter and Mary were in the front room of their new home. They had just finished a bottle of Sauvignon Blanc. Mary got up and put her arms around Peter and leant close.

'We've been saying we'll swim,' she said. Her breath on his cheek was warm and vinous. 'So come on, let's do it.'

In their Crocs and dressing gowns they crossed the road and went through the gap. Overhead tumbling clouds, but on the beach utter stillness

Mary took off her dressing gown and laid it over the edge of the boat. With no swimsuit she was round and heavy breasted and very white.

'What!' said Peter.

'You think they can see?' She waved at the farmhouse on the far side. 'The lake's ours, well half ours. I can do what I want.'

Mary waded out until the water was up to her knees, then she began to wet her body to acclimatise. Finally, she dropped down and began to swim, her head held high. 'Dowager stroke,' she called it.

He undid his dressing gown and was about to take it off when he spotted, in the trees on the other side of the boat, some bouquets in spattered wrappers.

'Why do people leave flowers?' he shouted.

Mary turned on her back. 'What?'

'Why do people leave flowers?'

'What are you talking about?'

He heard a bird beating its wings on the water and other

birds singing. There were many birds here – he sensed them everywhere – leading rich, invisible lives.

'There are old bouquets under the trees,' he shouted.

'To mark where someone died?' Mary suggested. 'An accident on the road?'

He wasn't sure. If they were killed on the road, shouldn't these have been on the hard shoulder? But then perhaps they were until someone threw them into the trees?

'Come on scaredy-cat,' she called. 'Your wife's waiting. Nothing's going to bite you.'

Briefly, he saw the vegetable box in the sink in the Camden Street kitchen, the rat's tail lashing against the white porcelain.

He laid his dressing gown on hers, then went out into the lake. Underfoot, he felt mud and sludge and leaf mould and rotting vegetation. Once the brown water was up to his thighs, he toppled forwards. He went right under, then lifted his head out and began to swim. The water felt slippery, quite different to the sea. He went to Mary. She was treading water and he slipped his arms around her from behind. She reached back.

'Any stirrings?' she asked.

A donkey brayed somewhere – he'd noticed it was hard to know exactly where sounds came from in the country – and he heard, momentarily, the high-pitched screech and the scrabbling of paws on the sink's floor as the rat struggled to get out from under the box.

Mary turned in the water to face him.

'Did I feel something?' She reached down.

'I doubt it,' he said. 'It's very cold.'

He remembered her fierce kiss in the Camden Street kitchen. He was a lifesaver, she'd said, hadn't she?

'This is our new beginning,' she said. 'And from now on we're swimming every day.'

And they did, Mary always without a costume, though Peter kept his on. He never felt sure they were absolutely alone in the water, though he never told her this.

———————

'My car needs its MOT,' said Mary.

Peter asked the postman if he knew a good mechanic. 'Vincent,' said the postman, 'and he won't be sore on your pocket.'

Vincent was in the village three miles away. Peter rang him and arranged to call.

In the village, stretched between the lamp posts, there were Orange arches showing King Billy on his charger and red, white and blue bunting. The Protestant church had flags flying from its tower. The Catholic church, in contrast, had nothing.

Peter found Vincent's, parked and got out. There was a white house and a corrugated shed with its doors open; inside, two men in a pit worked on a car's undercarriage using bright work lights.

Peter approached and waved. A bearded man, mid-sixties,

climbed out of the pit, leaving the other, a young lad with bright red hair, to work on.

The bearded man came up. 'I'm Vincent and the fella doing the real work is Davy.' He lit a cigarette and leafed through Mary's logbook. Then he started with the same questions about Peter and Mary's seed and breed as everyone else asked. Peter answered happily. As a blow-in he had to reply. He knew that. Then he asked a few questions of his own, which was also part of the ritual.

'Lough Coin,' he said, 'did you ever swim in it?'

'Not since I was a cub,' said Vincent.

'When was that?'

'Nineteen sixty something.'

'Long time ago?'

'Long time ago.'

Vincent's tone had changed. And his shoulders.

'The lake must be full of fish,' continued Peter. 'Never see a fisherman though.'

'Well,' said Vincent, 'when you can drive to the sea in an hour, why'd you stay around here? Let me get my diary.'

He went away and Peter wondered what the sea had to do with it. He couldn't work it out.

Vincent came back. 'I'll book the MOT,' he said. 'Bring the car Thursday, nine a.m. sharp. I'll drop you home and when all's redd up, I'll get the car to you and you drive me back. That's how we do it. The country way.'

When he got home later, rather than going up to the house Peter pulled on to the hard shoulder and went through to the beach. He saw ducks at the water's edge and swans further out. He saw dragonflies and something bright and frenzied that he presumed was a kingfisher. It struck him that without people, nature flourished on Lough Coin in a way he'd never seen anywhere else.

It was the third day of heat. Mary threw her dressing gown on the rotted boat and began to apply sunscreen.

'Ambre Solaire,' said Peter sniffing. 'The smell of summer.'

The abandoned bouquets caught his eye. They had cards stapled on. Might something be written on these? He went to see. Any writing that had been there was washed away, with the exception of one, on which he could just make out in faint print – *Quigley's of Newry*.

'I think all these bouquets are from the one florist,' he said. 'All the cards are the same size.'

'I'd say florists use a standard-sized card,' said Mary. 'Now stop with the sleuthing and come here.'

He threw off his dressing gown and went to her.

'Close your eyes.'

She sprayed his face, ears, shoulders, arms and legs. Then she rubbed in the suncream in her typical deft way.

'Done,' she said when she'd finished. She kissed him warmly, turned and crossed the hot coarse sand to the water's edge.

'You're getting an all-over tan,' he said. It was true. She was.

'Peter,' she said. 'What do you think that is?' She pointed.

It was a box of unusual dimensions, just under the surface. 'And how come I never noticed it?' she continued.

He hauled it out. It was metal, rusted and pockmarked with holes, out of which a brown glop that reminded him of Mrs Smyth's oxtail soup now poured. The lid was corroded shut. He hadn't the tools, he thought, to open it. Then he remembered. He was bringing Mary's car to Vincent the next morning. He'd ask him.

Punctually, Peter parked in front of Vincent's shed, pulled the boot release and got out. Vincent was in the pit with Davy. He clambered up the ladder and came out of the shed.

'I'm hoping you can open this,' said Peter.

Vincent peered into the boot. 'Out of the lake, was it?'

'Yes,' said Peter.

'Full of water, was it?'

'Yes, filthy brown stuff.'

'Good. I wouldn't touch it otherwise.' His tone and shoulders were altered exactly like before when they'd talked about Lough Coin.

They carried the box into the workshop and set it on a bench. Vincent found a wedge and a mallet and, after a lot of thumping, he got the lid off. Inside the box was full of sludge and packed with corroded casings out of each of which something dark and pointed stuck up. Vincent pulled one out and stood it up.

'Remember these?'

Peter did. The last time he had seen one it was lying in a gutter at the bottom of the Grosvenor Road and he was holding a handkerchief over his mouth and his eyes were weeping from the CS gas. It was a rubber bullet.

Vincent drove Peter home in his Toyota pick-up with the box on the flat-bed behind. The August light was dark and autumnal, yet it was warm too, and still summery. The seasons seemed to be mixed up. It began to rain. The windscreen wiper went on and the water drops smeared. Vincent smelt of Swarfega, Peter noticed.

They reached the house but instead of turning up the drive Vincent stopped on the hard shoulder by the lake, opened the window and lit a cigarette.

'This fella,' said Vincent, 'lived … lives … about a mile down the road there.' He waved ahead. 'A B-man, he joins the UDR, 1970, and he ends up in charge of the army stores in town. Now he's the light-fingered sort, unless it's nailed down … you get me? He starts to help himself … tyres, bandages, bullets, spades … anything he can lay hold of, and he takes it and sells it, or donates it to his side. Course he's rumbled. So what does the idiot do before the Redcaps visit? He takes everything stolen he has at home – and he has tons – and he dumps it in the lake in the middle of the night. Course they hear ...' Vincent waved at the farmhouse on the other side of the lake. 'And that's when they put up that fence to keep their animals away from the water.'

He drew on his cigarette and exhaled.

'And was that,' said Peter, 'after the stuff was dumped, when your father stopped you swimming, and the fisherman stopped coming?'

'Yeah, it was. Now, Peter, I know what you're thinking.' Vincent jerked his thumb at the flatbed behind where the box of rubber bullets sat. 'Yes, now and then some washes up. But it's been almost fifty years. The water has everything well spoiled by now. So I wouldn't worry. You can swim away in that to your heart's content.'

They talked on along these lines. By the time they finished Peter was persuaded. He made a mental note, however, to tell Mary they should keep their Crocs on when they swam. Just to be sure.

———

Peter woke very early on the morning of his birthday. He lay in bed listening to Mary breathing. He was wide awake. It was a bright day beyond the curtains. He dressed quietly and slipped out to the front doorstep. The lake below was a shining black plate, smooth and still. The sky, overlaid with a veil of white, was pale blue. There was a chill now but it would be warm once the sun got up. They'd have breakfast outside.

There was a fuchsia bush beside the door. Peter heard the drone of bees. He turned and watched one bee after another nosing into the red trumpet-like flowers. He was sixty-five and it was the start of his retirement. He felt good. Life was good. As he finished this thought he heard a cry – it sounded desperate – and a splash.

He turned and scanned the water. Nothing. He hurried down to the beach. In the distance, seven swans, white and regal; closer by, moorhens moving briskly. A fish jumped. He heard the tiny splash as it plopped back in. Then silence. There was nobody in sight.

But had he heard something? Yes, he had. Maybe it hadn't come from the lake. In the country, sounds never came from where you thought. In the country, a dog barking behind could easily sound as if it was barking in front. But he had heard something. Oh yes, he had.

———————

'You'll have to come and see this,' said Mary.

He was at the outside sink washing the rubber bullets clean.

He followed her to the front. On the hard shoulder opposite their drive stood a van, 'Newry Cabs' painted on the driver's door. The huge sliding door behind was open and someone was bringing a wheelchair out backwards and rolling it down a ramp, while another man with a bouquet stood watching.

Once the chair reached the ground, it was turned. Peter

saw an old woman was sat in it. He saw who was pushing too. He recognised the red hair.

'That's Davy who works with Vincent,' he said.

'And now you know who brings the flowers,' said Mary. 'Her.'

Davy trundled the old woman round the front of the taxi.

'So here's my thinking, Watson,' said Mary, 'Bloke on a Honda, her son, husband, fiancé, brother, son I'd say, doing a hundred, comes off here, into the lake, dies.'

Peter remembered the scream and the splash he heard earlier. Maybe Mary was on to something, he thought.

'That'd explain the flowers in the trees,' he said.

'Exactly,' she said. 'I'm good aren't I?'

Davy disappeared through the gap with the chair, followed by the other man, who was obviously the taxi driver. The visitors were on the beach now, out of sight.

'I've just had the most ghoulish idea,' said Mary. 'If we think what happened, happened today, which maybe it did, then we'll always see this on your birthday?'

'Why not?' he said. 'Every day has births *and* deaths.'

'Oh very sage,' said Mary.

Later, after the taxi left and Mary went to Tesco's, Peter went down to the beach. The new bouquet was standing against a tree. There was a card with a message written in Biro and this one he could read. *Darling Francie. Keep up the good work, Mam, XXXX.*

———————

It was raining, the spears heavy and thick. Peter jumped out of his car and sprinted into the workshop. The radio was on and in the pit, below the jeep parked above, the compressor gun thumped away.

He dropped to his hunkers and shouted, 'Hello!' into the pit.

Davy, further away, had the compressor and didn't hear but Vincent, who was closer, turned. When he saw it was Peter something showed on his face. He clambered up the ladder. The racket was deafening.

'I thought I'd be seeing you,' shouted Vincent. He indicated Davy then waved his finger as if to say 'no talking'. Then he shouted, pointing the other way, 'House.'

They jogged over in the rain to a side door. Vincent bolted in first; Peter followed.

'Fierce rain,' said Vincent, wiping his face.

They were in the kitchen. There was a Child of Prague on a lace doily on a shelf, a table with a bottle of Paddy and an old range with a Pulley Maid overhead from which a stiff tea towel hung.

'I suppose you minded our Davy the other day,' Vincent said.

'I did.'

'Course you did.'

'He was with a lady in a wheelchair.'

'Yeah. Tea?'

Peter nodded.

Vincent turned on the electric kettle and ran the sink tap. The water dunned on the bottom. He scrubbed his hands with a nail brush. The process was noisy. Peter sat though he hadn't been invited to. Vincent pulled the tea-towel down and dried his hands. A tin of biscuits appeared, minus its lid. Vincent sat. The kettle rumbled on.

'That lady you saw,' said Vincent, 'she's Davy's great aunt. She's in a nursing home in Newry, but when she comes home Davy helps her and that. Him and his folks are the only family she's left here.'

'And who's Francie?'

'Ah, that'd be her cub.'

'And what happened him? Was he killed in an accident?'

'No.' Vincent made quotation marks in the air. 'Informer. Allegedly. Not long after the dumping I was telling you about … Francie's tried by the RA, standard bollocks, then they row Francie out very early … tie his hands, tie him to this huge stone and heave him in.'

The kettle clicked off.

'And his mother comes on the anniversary?'

'She would, yeah, on the day.'

Vincent got up and returned with two mugs of tea. He unscrewed the bottle and poured whiskey into each.

'Was the body ever … ?'

'Oh yes. The army sent a frogman. There's a grave but it's the lake she minds.'

Outside the rain could be heard drumming on the cars parked around Vincent's house and on the shed roof. In the background the compressor was thumping away.

'She left flowers,' said Peter.

'Always does.'

The message said, 'Keep up the good work.'

'That'd be Bernie for you.'

A sudden wind hurled spatters on the windows and shook the glass.

'What did she mean?'

The room had gone dark. Vincent got up and turned on the light.

'Now and then some washes up … some of the stuff that was dumped. You know yourself. And it's Francie. Well Bernie thinks so. Always has. He's cleaning the lake out. That's what she thinks.'

'But,' began Peter and stopped.

'I know, but it keeps her happy.' Vincent shook the tin. 'Go on. Have a Hobnob. Spoil yourself.'

By the time Peter drove home the rain had stopped, the sun was back and here and there clouds of steam could be seen rising from the tarmac. Later, it got hot again.

That night, Peter stood in his living room with the lights off, staring out. The lake was liquorice, the sky inky.

Nothing was straight, he thought. It was spiralled. That's why he could be in the now while simultaneously squeezing Mr Smyth's ashes, or standing over the sink with the rat's tail flailing, or squinting at the spent rubber bullet in the gutter. And that was why the dead never died. They just went over there a bit. You couldn't see them but you could hear them and they could hear you.

The room grew darker. He'd have to turn the lights on, he thought, so Mary could see her way in. She was at her French conversation class. Home soon though.

Now, standing thinking about turning on the lights but not actually doing it, he remembered something she'd said. They had this house, she'd said, in the middle of nowhere, so any room, any room at all, he could take off her clothes and they could … that's what she'd said. The move down had stirred something that had been quiescent for years. Yes, he thought, he could give her a glass of wine when she got back and then he could give it a go.

Mary came home and he gave her the glass and a second and then he undressed her and they lay down on the floor in the front room and when they finished they were in absolute blackness and not a sound could be heard from the lake. But then the window was double-glazed, so that didn't mean anything.

'Dip?' she said. 'I bet the water's still warm.'

In his head Peter saw Francie in the murk lugging something ... No, he thought, best not to interrupt his work tonight.

'In the morning,' he said, 'we'll swim in the morning, promise.'

The Missing Girl
Extracts from an Oral History

Reggie Chamberlain-King

BORDER Lines is an ongoing oral history project of undetermined length. The following is a small part of a subset of what may be collected. Its inclusion here does not mean exclusion from the whole. Commentary is author's own, except where otherwise stated or implied.

———————

Two towns: **Bancarrick** *and* <u>Carrigbawn</u>. *With two churches: St Methodius's and St Cyril's. And two girls.*

One is kept from the other – the towns – by an untended field and four green hillocks, equally spaced apart. Give or take. The mounds funnel the wind across the field, from one town to the other or at a right angle to both. It is a through-line. Or it is a plane of symmetry, where one side reflects the other: <u>Carrigbawn</u> *and* **Bancarrick**. *Although, it's hard to say which one is the mirror's surface and which the black behind it.*

Moira Breen (Breen's, Bancarrick): The town is lovely, so it is.

Mary Byrne (Parish Secretary, St Methodius's, Carrigbawn): It's a lovely town.

Patsy Dunne (Whiterock Taxis): I do be over and back a fair bit – I'll not say why – so I've seen both sides.

Mike McGarrity (Bancarrick): Never heard of it.

Mary Byrne: I can see them from that front window, through the hills, across the field, all day long sometimes and more, when there's a stretch in the evenin'.

Moira Breen: But we keep ourselves to ourselves and wouldn't be givin' ourselves away.

Margaret McGoldrick (childhood friend): We wouldn't have much to do with them. Except for similar customs, shared history, and speech.

Mike McGarrity: The May Queen festival is unique to Bancarrick, right in the middle of when we're doin' the lambin'. The wee girl is picked from all the Communion girls that May.

Mary Byrne: And she's called the Bealtaine Belle and the men put her in a trap that's all covered in flowers and it's pulled by the donkey that won the Carrigbawn Cup, that's the Dooley Cup. Now, the Dooleys … they say they're the oldest family …

Mike McGarrity: And she's paraded past the church on this yoke. And the priest falls in behind.

Mary Byrne: And he leads them on to the cemetery, singin'.

Patsy Dunne: 'When in Death my eyes are closin', When the Winter is reposin', When my frame by death is broken, The Queen of Spring is re-awoken.'

Mike McGarrity: There was nothing like it hereabouts. That's ours.

Mary Byrne: Now we don't be doing that now this long an' long.

Moira Breen: Not for donkey's years now.

Margaret McGoldrick: She was a lovely wee gersha. She used to sit at the desk in front of me. She was a good un … she always broke her sandwich in half – dead precise – and gave a bit to Marion Dooley, because the Dooleys didn't have much. But Marion was okay.

Moira Breen: We wouldn't ah been pals, but I knew her of course. Everyone knew her, in the town.

Margaret McGoldrick: Awh, it's awful sad what happened.

Patsy Dunne: Just gone. Just like that. The both of them. You see, I knew that, because I'd be back and forth a lot and I know people. They were just gone, so they were.

<u>Margaret McGoldrick</u>: I thought it was a fox. It put the shit outta me. This god awful scream! My heart went crossways. It was comin' from the other side ah town. Maura Boyle, just screamin'. Deep out of 'er belly screamin'.

Fr John Donnan (Parish Priest, St Cyril's Church, Bancarrick): Sean was battering my door. Just the look of him – I remember that – like a dog on a chain. It wasn't late at that point, maybe ten, late enough, I suppose, but it was a long evening. He was just barking, 'She's gone. She's gone.'

Mike McGarrity: He was a proud man, Sean Boyd. But he was more father than man.

Fr Donnan: I didn't know who he meant at first – I'd taken her Confession just before tea ... Well, no I can't tell you that ... I wouldn't remember anyway ... Wee girl stuff.

<u>Margaret McGoldrick</u>: But then she was so composed. Her face was all red, like, but she wasn't afraid. She just started telling people what they needed to be doing.

Moira Breen: You wouldn't ah spoke to the Brits for fear ah somebody seein' yah speak to the Brits. And once you were saw, someone would say, so that was that, you'd be over. So you'd say just nothin' and there'd be nothin' to say.

<u>Mary Byrne</u>: And sure what would the guards do?

<u>Margaret McGoldrick</u>: She had people with sticks, getting into lines, beating out the grass. We'd wait ... one, two, three ...

listen out for her. We'd call out: 'Muireann!' … one, two, three … Three steps forward – beat the grass – 'Muireann!'

Mike McGarrity: He was away like a mad thing. I don't think he'd a plan at all, Sean.

Here's an exhaustive list of places that the parties would have looked for the two missing girls, Muireann and Máire: the graveyard, which is in the church grounds; the cemetery, which is not; the play park; the school yard; the bunscoil; the old abandoned mill; the remnants of the forge; the fork in the road; the bridge into town; Breen's Fancy Goods; McCreesh's, the garage; McCreesh's, the shop; McCreesh's, the undertakers; the parochial houses; the chip shops; the Welcome Inn; O'Hara's; O'Leary's; McKibben's; The Red Devil Bar. And, later, the shebeens.

Cllr Manny Given (County Councillor, Bancarrick District): I was just walking home – now, I had a coupla drinks in me, not a skinful. I'd one Guinness, two whiskeys, that's all I ever have. Even on Christmas Day, that's all I ever have, and it was only startin' to get dark. There was a bit of a stretch in the evening, because it was May … what, a week ago, I'd put the crown upon her wee head: the wee Queen of the May. Sweet wee thing. That was just a week before. I couldn't believe it. I was walking home just, through the town, and I heard this shoutin' – wild shoutin' – and it wasn't coming from the village.

Fr Donnan: On the scrubland there.

Margaret McGoldrick: Between two hillocks.

Cllr Given: The roars of Sean Boyd, the roars of him. So I ran out there and the wind was cutting through and I only saw a black form – like two men fightin'. Sean Boyd, he's on this lad and he's batin' him and batin' him. Now, I take my civic duty pretty serious, when it counts, so, y'know, I was gonna keep an eye on how this developed. The two of them was just rollin' around and I remember – and this is clear as day – he was shoutin', 'No, that's our girl. She's ours.'

Malachy Boyle (Muireann's cousin): And he was hittin' me, just blow after blow, and I didn't know why. And I had a stick and everything. I'd been working forward through the field and he'd been walking towards me and, when we met, in the middle, he said, 'Have you seen our girl?' and he showed me this photo, but it was her: it was our Muireann.

Patsy Dunne: Now, I know this, being forward and back so much, but the photo in the *Sentinel* and the photo in the *Advocate*: they were the same girl. Different names, but the same girl.

> Police are appealing for information after a young girl went missing in the border town of Bancarrick over the weekend.

The 8-year-old, Máire Boyd, was last seen at approximately 7.30 p.m. on Saturday evening, 8 May. Máire is described as white, 5ft 1in tall, slim build with blonde, shoulder-length hair. Police believe she is wearing a light summer dress, white jelly shoes, and she may have had a crown of flowers upon her head. The family is desperate to hear news of anyone matching this description.

Bancarrick Sentinel,
10 May 1976

<u>Margaret McGoldrick</u>: She never took it off that week. She was so proud: the Belle. She was the Belle … She still is.

<u>Mary Byrne</u>: She (Maura Boyle) never gave up hopin'. She never gave up prayin'. She was at the Mass every day, not like these other ones kissin' the altar rails. She was organisin' searches and posters … great big posters. They were up for years. Or she kept puttin' up new ones.

Mike McGarrity: I always thought, sure she'd be older now. But maybe not, y'know?

Fr Donnan: That did for him, I think. looking out across the way and seeing all them posters looking back, on the lamp posts, dangling off the bridge. They weren't for the benefit of their town, they all seemed to be pointing out, towards our town. His daughter's face. You couldn't blame him for turning in on himself.

Patsy Dunne: There wasn't much traffic now, that's true. And I would know. Not much talk of what was happenin' over there or what was happenin' over here. It was cold between 'em for quite some time. I'd say it was only the wind sometimes that went from one to the other.

Cllr Given: Certainly, I considered it my job, as a public representative, to consider doing something. And I did. I considered it long and hard.

Moira Breen: You'd see Sean slopin' about a bit, but he was a beaten man. Then, after a while, I didn't see him in the shop much. After a while, you don't ask as much as you did.

<u>Margaret McGoldrick</u>: I don't know how she kept her energy. I didn't think I'd ever see Muireann back again, so I don't know how her ma kept her faith in all that. You just do, I suppose. Something like that: it's a such a big thing to lose, like – your baby, your child – you'd just hold on to it for as long as you could. You give up and that's you choosin' to keep them missing.

Fr Donnan: I think he'd have been happy for either of the girls to be found. He'd have let the other ones take her too. Y'know, a different name, a different family, but she'd be alive. He'd know she was alive.

<u>Margaret McGoldrick</u>: I called my first one Muireann, so

there'd be a wee Muireann runnin' about.

Mike McGarrity: You'd see the siblings about – all boys, ginger. Mick Boyd was a good lad. I played at the hurlin' with him. But you didn't see the da about at all, not in the end.

Patsy Dunne: Sure yuh hear rumours. I mean, I do, as I'm in and out all the time. It's a wee place. Or they're both wee places, y'know. But somebody knows something. Or, at least, somebody says something. Everybody says something. Not out loud, like.

Moira Breen: When is this goin' out?

I don't know.

Moira Breen: Not soon?

No.

Moira Breen: Well ... don't say that I said, but the dogs in the street know it ... I heard they found the body ... they were bound to eventually ... there was always someone in that field then. But it was just the one body.

Whose body?

Fr Donnan: I can't tell you anything about that.

Cllr Given: No, I can't confirm that. The border would be outside my jurisdiction. Needless to say that if our lovely young May Queen had been found, it would have been made known. I would not have been shy in sheddin' a tear for Máire Boyd. I have shed many a tear for that poor girl. That poor missing girl. Our May Queen *in perpetua*.

Patsy Dunne: There would have been ructions. You know it. After what your one Boyd was like the last time, what do you think he'd be at? I can tell ya: 'No, that's your one! The dead one's your one.' Would you accept the dead child? Or would you hold out for the living one? Like a gameshow: 'Do you wanna take the money or open the box?'

Margaret McGoldrick: It was never filled – that desk, in school. I'd think about it though, all the way through school, because, y'know, there was the one classroom, so I was in there until I went to the big school. Missin' her. Picturin' her break that sandwich in half and giving Marion Dooley her bite. And y'know what kids are like! There were stories. Like they'd found a body and the Brits came down from the barracks and sorted them all out. They'd cut her in half, like Solomon did – that was the only way to settle it. And the parent that would give the child up, whole, that's the one who was the real parent. That's how they would identify her, what with the two girls looking the same.

And which parent was that? Maura Boyle or Sean Boyd?

Margaret McGoldrick: They said they just took what they were given and went home happy. But they wouldn't do that. That's just kids' talk.

Malachy Boyle: Auntie Maura never gave up. The house was just full of stuff … pictures … toys … she never got rid of any of it. She was happy as long as she was trying. But she tired herself out. She was always going to. I think that, if she'd rested, she would have died. And so she worked herself to death. […] Yes, we buried her out in the scrub there. We think that's what she would have wanted. […] Whose permission would we need? It's nobody's.

Mike McGarrity: Aye, Boyd's house was near empty. This was at Sean's wake. They never had one for Máire. The blinds were shut, but, then, he always had them shut. That's your metaphor right there – you can have that fer nuthin'.

Patsy Dunne: There's ones over there wouldn't trust ones over here.

Margaret McGoldrick: No, it wasn't the same again. Corny as that sounds.

Cllr Given: You'd like to resurrect the old traditions. Maybe claim back some of that from the tragedy. It might do the place good. But I don't know if I could do it – not yet. If they want somethin' new, they can elect someone else. [*laughs*]

Fr Donnan: 'When in Death my eyes are closin', When the Winter is reposin', When my frame by death is broken, The Queen of Spring is re-awoken.'

The Wink and the Gun

John Patrick Higgins

I had to deliver a birthday present to a friend, a book I'd wrapped in brown paper and secured with string rather than Sellotape. It was a book on British Maritime History. We'd once had a conversation on the subject and I thought she seemed interested. Her name was Catherine and I hadn't known her very long, so I hoped I'd read the situation correctly. I slipped the package through her letterbox and listened to it crash on to the tiled hallway, before going on my way.

She lived on bohemian Oakland Avenue in the east of the city. It was a street of brightly coloured doors and children's wellingtons left on designer doormats. Fiat 500s bit into the pavements, so I walked down the middle of the road. There was nobody about.

At the end of the street was a sturdy, pebble-dashed Scout Hall, the grey of dry pumice. Next to the barred windows swung a sign in a curling wrought-iron brace, artisanal in a way the street's occupants wouldn't recognise. The sign was weather-beaten into inarticulacy but retained a naïve drawing of a tepee. The hall's doors were boarded up and two of the three unprotected windows were cracked and held in place with ancient orange tape. It was so odd: flat-roofed and hand-moulded, a strange projection of the past into the present – something boxy and unlovely squatting in this metropolitan street. I wondered if it was still in use.

As I reached the Newtownards Road I turned right. I was going to visit the local shopping centre and pick up some contact lenses. It was my only reason for going there and I never enjoyed the visit, but Oakland Avenue was equidistant between my house and Connswater and, besides, it was a sunny day and I had to pick them up at some point.

I was brought up in east Belfast, but lived elsewhere for many years. My job took me all over the world – I was a cameraman for sporting events – so it didn't much matter where I lived as long as it was near an airport. At the age of forty, I returned to the city, taking advantage of the house prices: you get a lot of brick for your buck in Northern Ireland.

I rarely left the house when at home. The city centre was completely foreign to me. I didn't know the good pubs and restaurants or if there were any. I kept my head down.

The natives of Belfast are gregarious and affectionate, though if you say that to people who haven't been here they don't believe you. They are a soulful, gentle people. Equally, they are loud, community-minded and interested in your business, and I'm not like that. I keep myself to myself. I don't have any family left. I'm just me, not rooted but stuck in the mud – buying contact lenses, but not making eye contact.

As a child I enjoyed sport: I wasn't good at it, but I liked the rules. They were exact, impartial, and invented by stern Victorians. Rules were good. Rules were fair. My other interest was photography. It was solitary and quiet and played to my strengths: my separateness and my tireless collecting of kit. Everything reassuringly black and white. There was magic in birthing something new in a chemical tray in the cupboard under the stairs. So I travelled the world photographing sport and when I was at home, I stayed at home.

Connswater was one of the few places I did visit. It was an unlovely warren of discount perfumeries, pound shops, and army recruitment stands. The top tier was all fast food outlets and toilets, the one suggesting the other in a joyless, nutrition-free exchange. The building was large and rectangular, except for a glass and metal rupture at the entrance, bulging like a swollen belly and pressed bullishly against the multistorey opposite. Pylons bristled like Titans as cars beetled between their splayed legs. Everyone was on their phones, walking at a zombie's pace. There was no urgency – just grumbling, low-level menace. I hated this place, but my optician was here and I needed my lenses. I had a school reunion I didn't want to attend but probably would, and I couldn't imagine going in my specs.

Connswater was full of children, gangs of them, sharp as splinters, faces hard with purpose. They laughed and jostled and swore, but had a seriousness and self-possession that terrified me. They had the compact energy of seeds about to violently bloom. I kept my distance. Well, you have to nowadays.

I picked up a month's worth of contact lenses from the smiling optician and I was out the door in minutes, swinging my branded plastic bag and happily free of the crowds, the dusty shells of dead shops, the persistent smell of hot fat.

I thought I would walk home along the Comber Greenway. The Greenway had been the route of the Belfast and County Down Railway for a hundred years until it was dismantled in the 1950s. It malingered, always on the cusp of becoming something for a further half century. Finally it was resurfaced and rebranded as a tranquil green corridor providing local people with a *'traffic-free route for walking or cycling'*. It is seven miles of meandering valley, with soft verges rising on both sides. It's chiefly used by joggers, cyclists, and dog-walkers, the latter marking their territory with black bags of animal waste, hung from the branches of trees like foul Christmas decorations. Still, on a fine day, it was preferable to the exhaust fumes and graffiti of the main road. I headed past the trolley bay and crossed over to Bloomdale Street, a short terrace of houses with the usual proliferation of Union flags sagging in front. Cigarette butts formed fairy circles next to

—

cars parked on the pavements. Down an entry a shopping trolley looked guilty.

A woman walked towards me with a Bichon Frise on a short leash. She was wearing sportswear in a manner which suggested she didn't always wear sportswear. Her black hair was scraped back from her face, which was thinner than the last time I had seen it, her eyebrows fuller and darker. But there was no mistaking her. It was Tanya Millar. Tanya Millar from school. I hadn't seen her for a quarter of a century and she looked great.

'Tanya?' I said. She turned sharply, her eyes narrowing as she flicked through some mental Rolodex. Her eyes widened with her smile.

'McCullagh! For goodness sake,' she said.

'What are you doing here?' I asked.

'I've been walking my dog, what do you think? This is Beattie.' The dog jumped up and sniffed my groin in a friendly manner.

'What are *you* doing here?' she asked, 'I heard you moved away.'

I confirmed I had moved away, but was now back. She looked at me with her large, dark eyes. She was twenty years older and her hair hadn't always been that colour, but she'd aged beautifully. I occasionally bumped into my male classmates on my short sorties to the shops and time appeared to have made an example of them, but not her.

'How long has it been?' she said.

'Shut up!' she replied when I told her. 'I can't be that old. You can't. We're too good-looking.'

I laughed. I could think of nothing to say but I was pleased to have made a noise, just to join in.

'Are you going to the reunion?' she said.

It seemed more than likely.

'I might see you there. I've got to run on here, but I might see you there. Fancy that – Ol' Blue Eyes is back.'

I enjoyed watching her jog off down the street and I thought back to school: I'd always liked her, but never did anything about it. She barely spoke to me then. But, twenty years on, she remembered my name and thought I was good-looking. She specifically reminded me to attend our school reunion. It was all very exciting.

She had come through a gap in the wall leading out to the Greenway. The red paint on the wall looked like it had been touched up several times, but had never properly taken. Its lividity spread in patches and odd mineral clumps were pressed into it. It looked like the rusting hull of a land-locked trawler. The stone was bitten into and the gap seemed broken away, snapped off like a tooth, sharp as coral.

My mind was still racing from meeting Tanya Millar as I approached the wall and passed through. I felt slightly drunk. I had to admit I was lonely. I never went out as I had no one to see and nothing to do. This brief meeting had changed everything. It had opened up Belfast for me. The sky was suddenly a magnificent blue. Perhaps I could be happy in this city. It was, after all, my home. I could go to pubs, to restaurants, anywhere. I could start to live. I could learn to love Belfast.

As I climbed the dirt path on the other side of the gap, something unexpected pushed into view: a familiar object rendered unfamiliar. The light suddenly changed, the landscape pulled out of joint, as though I had stumbled into the prestige of a magic trick without seeing the set-up. The canopy of trees over the Greenway was no longer there. Instead a crude, wooden ziggurat had landed like Dorothy's house in Oz, sudden and strange. It was thirty feet high and neatly constructed of slatted wooden pallets. It was a bonfire, a Twelfth bonfire. And it was April.

It shouldn't have been there and the shock of its presence made me miss my footing. Tipping forward, my shopping spilled in front of me and my hands skidded across the pathway, skinning my palms and catching my left thumb awkwardly. The pain was sudden and sharp. I drew myself up to my knees and pushed the hand into my armpit. My thumb throbbed angrily. With my good hand, I returned the lenses to the bag and looked around to see if anyone had noticed. And that was when I saw the boys.

There were two of them, standing about five yards apart and staring at me. I was, maybe, thirty feet away, so they must have seen the whole thing. I could add embarrassment to the list of indignities. I got to my feet and dusted myself down with my good hand. The boys continued to stare. There was something odd about them, something I couldn't place. They just stood there, their faces expressionless.

I thought back to when I was their age, perhaps ten or eleven. If I had seen a flushed middle-aged man tripping over his own feet, holding an optician's carrier bag, I would have thought it hilarious. The cornerstone of all humour is a fat man falling and there was an added transgressive edge because I was an adult and I was belittled. *Schadenfreude* is sweeter when dignity is punctured and, to a child, a humiliated adult is the funniest thing of all.

But these two just stood there. They didn't react in any way. I sensed no aggression and I didn't feel they were trying to intimidate me. They just *stared*, as though I were something new that had stumbled into their world and for which they had no taxonomic reference.

There was something else. It didn't strike me then, not as a conscious thought, but occurred to me much later. I would have cause to reflect on the encounter at some length.

They didn't *look* like other children. The other kids in the area were tough and pinched, with tight haircuts and branded clothing. Their footwear was more expensive and better cared for than my own. They understood the value of presentation. Their style was performative, tied in with their aspirations and the larger ideas they wished to express about themselves.

These two boys betrayed no such information. They were spare-looking, under-nourished and hollow-eyed, and their hair was shaggy and grown out. They wore green woollen jumpers patched at the elbow and their jeans looked as if they'd known previous owners. It struck me that I hadn't seen a child wearing jeans in a very long time. Their gutties were laughably simple affairs: tiny coracles of rubber and canvas, the only decoration a Plimsoll line running the length of the shoe.

But it was their silence and stillness and the deadness of their eyes... Their faces were masks, revealing nothing. They didn't move, but their bodies seemed permanently on the point of doing so, coiled for action.

My left hand was still throbbing and, seeing no need to prolong our silent acquaintance, I began to move off down the Greenway. The moment I started to move the nearer boy moved too. His arm jerked at the elbow; his thumb and forefinger extended; his face creased into a heavy wink.

'Pow!'

He was giving me the wink and the gun. It was so strange and sudden that I started backwards, nearly stumbling again. I walked away, looking back several times before finally winding around a corner and losing sight of the boys. Every time I looked, he was still frozen in this strange attitude, gun pointed at me, his face still clearly contorted into a wink, long past the point I could make out individual features.

At home, I ran my thumb under the cold tap – it was stiff

but not hugely painful. There was some swelling, so I wrapped it in a dishcloth and took two paracetamol. I went to unpack the carrier bag and realised one of the boxes of lenses was missing. I checked the optician's initial on the remaining box: the squiggled 'L' meant the right eye lenses were gone. I could have gone back to the Greenway to look for them or I could have ordered more, but I was too excited. Tanya Millar looked amazing and I wanted to see if I could track her down on social media. I sat down in my office and switched on the computer when there was a loud rap at the door as though from a doorknocker, though I didn't have one.

Opening the front door, there was nobody there, but lying on the doormat was my packet of right eye contact lenses. The boys must have found them. They'd followed me home. They knew where I lived. I scooped up the box and looked about, but there was no sign of the boys anywhere in the street. The strangeness of our encounter shivered through me once again. Though really, what had happened?

I stared out of the living room window for a few minutes, watching the schoolchildren, their blazers at right angles to their bodies, their school bags trailing behind them like unloved pets. Joggers puffed past, the street echoing with their flat-footed slaps. The people who lived on my street were mostly old. They didn't have funky cars or *personality* front doors like the denizens of Oakland Avenue. They were neat and careworn and so were their houses. There was nothing strange in my world and there never had been until those boys had rattled me. I felt scolded by their seriousness and their silence, by the strange, sustained gesture of the wink and the gun. There was no cheek in it, no play: it felt like a warning, even a threat.

The thumb didn't get better. After a few weeks I went to the doctor who sent me to A&E. They sent me to get the thumb X-rayed and I finally spoke to a specialist who told me that it had broken and was already healing badly. They could rebreak it and pin it, but the damage looked irreversible and the middle joint in my thumb might never work again. And so it proved. They gave me a sandwich bag of blue putty, some plastic squares, and a photocopy of some physiotherapy exercises and that was it for my thumb. To this day it will not bend, but it doesn't hurt in the least.

About a month later, I put on my suit and tie and booked a cab for eight. It was the evening of the school reunion. I opened a bottle of wine and either sat or paced, occasionally passing the invitation on the kitchen counter.

By eight, the first bottle was finished, I had started on a second, and I realised that I was not going to go to the school reunion. Relief washed over me. I wouldn't have to humiliate myself in front of Tanya Millar and the rest of the school. I was risking disaster on a chance meeting in a local beauty spot. I had read too much into our minute-long exchange. I was being a fool. The taxi driver beeped outside at eight and my phone vibrated. I sank deep into my chair and listened to the taxi pull away, accelerating in anger.

I examined my face in the mirror over the mantelpiece and, in fact, I didn't look too bad with the wine-goggles on. I still had hair. I had money. I wasn't *too* fat and the suit looked pretty good. We would have been a viable couple. I really *should* have gone to the reunion. Of course Tanya would be there. She'd more or less invited me and, anyway, a few weeks of *minor* online stalking had revealed she was divorced and almost certainly a free agent. My research had been thorough. There was some unfinished business there or, at least, some not-yet-started business. I *had* to go – I could get another cab. And I would wear my contact lenses – give Tanya the benefit of my baby blues. 'Ol' Blue Eyes is back.'

I opened the box of right eye contact lenses and noticed a tiny hole had been made at the top of each sachet. In each of the thirty capsules a pinprick had allowed the saline to evaporate, the lenses hardened into brittle translucent molluscs. The boys had done it. It had all the hallmarks of schoolboy cruelty: the wantonness, the pointlessness, the sloppy execution. They would never see the outcome of their destruction, but they had destroyed. It was enough. But it wasn't *quite* enough. They had missed one. A single plastic bulb was still intact, its contents still workable. I tore away at the foil, removed the lens with a forefinger and, tilting my head back, pressed it on to my eye.

I had never known pain like it. It was immediate and searing, dizzyingly focused. My eyelid clamped down, the ruined eye filling with tears in an attempt to cushion this foreign body, to lift it free of the surface and wash it away. I pushed it around the eye, howling in torment, unable to switch off the penetrating agony. The lens felt like it was breaking into shards, puncturing the soft film, scraping it, scorching it. I could smell hot copper as I clawed my face, stumbling into the kitchen to push my eye under the tap, to flush away the pain, filling the sink with pale, roseate blood. Panicked, I stabbed 999 into my phone and vomited, my eye socket an open wound. I fainted, but came to in time to stagger to the door for the ambulance.

The doctors couldn't tell me what had happened or what kind of corrosive was on the lens. I lost the eye.

Catherine came to visit me in hospital to thank me for the book. She was shocked when she saw my face. 'My God,' she said, 'What will you do for a job?'

I laughed it off. 'I only need one eye to take photographs,' I said. I held my phone to my bad eye and took a picture of her. 'I see no ship.' She smiled, but clearly didn't get the reference. But, then, she was French, so there was no reason why she should.

I was discharged before the bandages came off, but a nurse would visit a couple of times a week to help with the dressing. I took to wearing an eyepatch when I went out. It wasn't worth it around the house.

I often went back to the Greenway. I traced the path I had taken that day. By then, it was the start of July and the bonfire was huge and densely populated with young, industrious ordinary people. Never the ones I was looking for. I saw no sign of Tanya either.

One day, there was a loud rap at the door. It sounded like someone slamming a doorknocker, though I don't have one. I answered and there they were: the boys. They looked exactly the same, same clothes, everything. They stood there, expectant and silent on my doorstep. I couldn't speak. Words would not come. I simply lifted my hand to point at them, gasping, my thumb rigid, the hollow of my ruined eye closed over and we three stood in the paralysed moment.

'Pow!' said the boy in front. They both started to laugh.

The Quizmasters

Gerard McKeown

CYCLING home that afternoon, my biggest concern was whether it might rain. I had just passed Glarryford, with a ten-mile ride ahead of me back to Ballymena. Wished I'd taken a coat, like Mum had suggested. As a muddy old Ford Fiesta crawled up on the left of me, I thought I felt the first spit of rain. *There* was a car that needed a good burst of rain. Would it be heavy enough to clean the dirt off it though? Also available in white, even though it was blue. I looked up at the heavy grey sky and waited for another spit.

'Excuse me,' the driver, a beardy-looking hippy in sunglasses that didn't suit the weather, said, leaning his head out of the window. 'Am I close to Ballymena?'

'Keep following this road,' I said to him. 'Turn left at the end and keep going straight. That'll take you into Carniny. That's you on the outskirts of Ballymena.'

'Very good,' he said. 'Is Liam Neeson from Ballymena?'

He had an English accent. This was the sort of question I'd

have expected from an American tourist, in a car too big for the road, honking at me *to get outta the frickin' way*.

'He is,' I said. 'There's no statue or anything though.'

'Can you name anyone else famous from Ballymena?' he said. Ballymena is an odd place for a tourist to go; it's not scenic, and there are no tourist attractions worth talking about.

'Eamonn Loughran? He was a world champion boxer. Not sure what his weight class was. Lost his belt there a couple of years ago and hasn't fought since.'

'Very good,' he said, like that was his catchphrase. 'What weight division did he fight in?'

'I just said I didn't know.'

'Well take a guess.'

I squeezed my brakes to stop. The hippy had his foot on the brake just as fast.

'Guess,' he said, not mentioning that we'd stopped.

'Welterweight?'

He motioned with his head at the road in front of us. I obediently began peddling at my previous speed. The Fiesta trundled alongside. The hippy stuck his head back in the window. That's when I clocked someone in the passenger seat. The driver stuck his head back out.

'Very good,' he said in an enthusiastic tone, as if he was a true TV quizmaster who could turn on the charm when the cameras were rolling, as if me stopping had been forgotten. 'Who's the MP for Ballymena?'

I knew where this was going; he was leading up to ask my religion. I could give the wrong answer, say I didn't know, but these two would make their own minds up anyway.

The best chance I'd have of getting away was if they stopped the car to get out. I'd throw the bike over the hedge and hope the field wasn't too bumpy to ride across.

'What's with your questions?' I said, hoping I could bait him into stopping the car.

Whoever was in the passenger seat said something to him, but I couldn't hear it.

'Do you know the answer?' the quizmaster asked.

'I might.'

'You look too young to vote. I don't think you know it. You might as well take a guess though.'

'Ian Paisley.'

'Very good,' he said. I'd half thought of giving him a wrong answer just to hear what his catchphrase would be then.

'Ballymena's not the name of the constituency,' he said. 'Do you know what that is?'

I noticed his accent slip when he said Ballymena. He pronounced it Ballamena, like a local would. He was from somewhere in Northern Ireland. His beard was probably fake too.

'Do you know this one?' he asked.

I did know, and I only knew because my dad insisted we watch the news every evening, at a time when my schoolfriends were watching *The Fresh Prince of Bel-Air*, *The Simpsons* or, fuck knows why, *Boy Meets World*. Dad loved to shout at the TV when some politician he didn't like was being interviewed.

'North Antrim,' I said.

'Very good,' he said. 'Be a bit quicker with your answers now. Quickfire. Quit this stalling. What party is Paisley the leader of?'

'The DUP.'

'Which stands for?'

'Democratic Unionist Party.'

'Very, very good,' he said, adjusting his catchphrase as if he knew it needed refreshing. 'Is politics a subject you know a lot about?'

'Not really,' I said, getting ready for them to jump out of the car. 'I keep myself pretty neutral.'

'That's sensible. Here's a sports one,' the quizmaster said, his accent slipping again. 'Who's the most capped player for Northern Ireland?'

'Surprised you're not asking me how to spell John.'

'Quick now. Do you know?'

'J-O-N.'

'Ha ha,' he said. 'Quit your time-wasting and answer *my* question.'

His tone when he said *my* implied an importance to the questions, something beyond this weird set-up, that I wouldn't be able to guess, and he wouldn't explain unless he had to.

In the distance I heard a tractor. At our speed, there was no way we were catching up to it; it must have been coming towards us. When they pulled aside to let it pass, that's when I'd jump the hedge into the field.

'Pat Jennings,' I guessed. Him and George Best were the only Northern Ireland players I knew.

The tractor, a big red Massey Ferguson, came puffing out the end of a lane and turned down the road away from us. Even at its slow speed it pulled quickly ahead. I turned back to the quizmaster, who'd been watching me watching the tractor. His grin seemed to acknowledge he'd known what I'd been thinking, as if he'd read the change of emotions on my face at every step of my failed plan, from hope to despair, through flickers of disappointment and anger as the tractor did the opposite of what I wanted it to. Needed it to.

The quizmaster ducked his head back into the car and spoke to the person on the passenger side. I tried to get a look at whoever was sitting there, but in the overcast afternoon, they were in shadow. I couldn't even make out their shape clearly, whether they were male or female.

'Very good,' the quizmaster said. 'It was Pat Jennings. Most people go for George Best.'

Most people? Had they done this before? I couldn't just wait to see where they were going with this. Next time he ducked his head back in, I was going to ride for it. I changed up a gear to make it easier to accelerate.

'What was that you did?' the quizmaster asked.

'That one of your questions?'

'If you like. You'd better give me the correct answer.'

'I changed gear. There's a bit of a hill coming up.'

'No there's not,' he said. 'Don't get any ideas about riding off.'

I maintained eye contact, without agreeing or disagreeing.

'We can do more than run you off the road,' he said.

I didn't want to ask what the more was, but the fact he had admitted this much, that running me off the road was an option, proved I was right to feel unsafe.

'What's your strong subject?' he asked, again in that friendly TV host tone.

'Dunno. Music, Films, TV shows,' I could hear in my voice that he'd shaken me.

The guy in the passenger seat said something to the quizmaster. I knew it was a guy by the tone of his voice, but I couldn't hear what he'd said.

'Okay,' the quizmaster said, sticking his head back out of the window. 'Who plays Joey Potter on *Dawson's Creek*?'

My surprise at being asked a question about something as unexpected as that silly show, snapped me momentarily out of the fear I'd been feeling, then plunged me back into it and held me down deeper. For the first time, my legs shook with adrenalin. I thought I was about to cry.

'What?' I said. My mouth was dry.

'Who plays Joey Potter on *Dawson's Creek*?'

I almost started to laugh. 'Katie Holmes.'

'Ten out of ten,' the quizmaster said. 'You're a lucky fella.'

'What?' I said, knowing as soon as I'd said it that I shouldn't have challenged him saying lucky.

The quizmaster glanced ahead of him. I realised he'd barely looked at the road since he pulled up beside me. The guy in the passenger seat must have been watching for oncoming traffic.

'Stay in school,' the quizmaster shouted before they sped off.

I squeezed my brakes and stopped abruptly. Without realising it was coming, I vomited over the handlebars. Stringy orange saliva hung from my mouth, strands of it resting in the treads of my front wheel.

A fresh wave of panic hit me, as I realised they might turn and come back. I cycled on, hoping to come across a house, a phone box. Somewhere I could tell someone. Somewhere I could feel safe. Only, I wasn't exactly sure what had just happened. Sure, the man had threatened me, or been threatening, by telling me they could run me off the road, or do more than that, and the mysterious guy in the passenger side had been creepy, but really what could I tell the police? They asked me some questions and drove off. I picked up speed, hoping not to see that muddy blue Fiesta coming back for me.

I heard the shot before I saw the body. I knew it was them. It didn't sound as far ahead as I'd expected, and even after the quizmaster had threatened me, I hadn't thought he'd meant with a gun. Even the suspicion of it would have sunk me so deep into fear, the shock of it would have killed me before they'd taken aim.

My shaking hands threatened to fly off the handlebars, but the danger of cracking my skull on the tarmac forced me to hold steady. I squeezed my brakes but going slower felt more uncertain. I started to peddle, then sped up, not processing why, or that I shouldn't. A wave of what I could only describe afterwards as morbid curiosity overcame the instincts that should have been protecting me. I felt strength in my arms as I gripped the handlebars. I didn't even slow down for the corner, and even though I took it as wide as possible, I almost came off the bike.

Again, another clear straight road stretched out in front of me. The combination of a signpost ahead, the clouds, and a distant house made the sight seem like a messed-up face. Like it was grinning or something. As if it was someone from the newly opened McDonald's in town wishing me to have a nice day.

In the road ahead I clocked a bike lying on its side, but no sign of the rider. I stopped beside it and looked around, wondering about the gunshot and if they'd taken the owner with them.

'Who plays Gunther in *Friends*?' a woman's voice said. 'Who plays Gunther in *Friends*?'

The voice sounded impatient. A body lay crumpled in the long grass beside the fallen bike. I stepped off my bike, laying it on the edge of the grass, and tried ignoring the unsteady feeling in my legs.

'Who plays Gunther in *Friends*?' the woman said.

I'm not sure if she noticed me, as she stared upwards at the heavy bags of potential rain crowding the sky. She was wearing a baggy top, like a waterproof jacket, black like a bin bag. I wasn't sure if I should touch her to feel for where she'd been shot. I'd heard you were supposed to put pressure on the bullet hole, or tie your shirt round it like in the films, but I froze with my hands held in front of me as if I was about to do something with them.

As my shadow hit her face, her eyes flicked but didn't connect with mine.

'Who plays Gunther in *Friends*?' she said, more frantic than before.

'I don't know,' I said. I could picture the actor who played him, his peanut-shaped head bright like a lightbulb, but I didn't have the first clue what his name was. That would have got me shot.

'Who plays Gunther in *Friends*?' the woman repeated, her voice sounding close to crying, her breath catching in her chest, like sobbing, as if she was dragging every breath into her lungs.

'Gunther,' she said, alternating with each breath. '*Friends.*'
'Gun,' she said, fighting for breath. 'Gun.'

I hadn't even time to make the connection before her speech dissolved further.

'Gu…' she said. 'Gu…'

The last attempt at a word caught in her mouth as the 'u' drew out into a long rattling exhalation. All sound from her stopped. Sirens were the next thing I heard. For all the good they did.

The police never caught The Quizmasters, as they came to be known. The details I gave the police were useless, a blue Ford Fiesta, very muddy. In my panic, I'd forgotten to note their number plate. Others did, and the plates were fake. As fake as the quizmaster's beard and English accent. There were three other survivors. Two passed the quiz, while another survived the shooting. There were five deaths in total, including the cyclist I'd witnessed. Because guns were involved, paramilitaries were suspected, but the different organisations all put out statements saying they weren't connected.

One local newspaper, in bad taste, printed the quiz questions from the survivors. I refused to speak to the paper, so they must have got mine from the police. I'd kept the question about Gunther to myself. Not telling the police, the woman's family when I went to her funeral, or the counsellor I saw afterwards when I started getting panic attacks every time I left the house. I didn't know who played Gunther and could have answered only a few of the questions put to the other survivors.

I couldn't watch *Friends* after that, and it's on everywhere, even still, though the series has long finished. That show will never die, first being repeated endlessly on Channel 4 for over a decade, to being repeated endlessly nowadays on Channel 5. After that, it will move to a smaller channel, something like Dave, or UK Gold. And I'll come across it when I'm channel-hopping, perhaps even seeing one of James Michael Tyler's 148 appearances as Gunther. I might even gather enough nerve to watch Gunther harmlessly long for Rachel, a girl he will never get. The character and the actor both innocent parties. Neither knowing their connection to the slaughter of three cyclists and two pedestrians between Coleraine and Ballymena on that unlucky overcast day.

That small secret nugget of knowledge being only mine, is the tiny, but present, burden I carry for not being able to hold that woman's hand, or offer her comforting words as she died, but also a reminder that I'm only here because of a small set of lucky questions.

Every time I flick on the television, the possibility of seeing Gunther haunts me.

Redland

Aislínn Clarke

I T started with the dog, snapping and snarling through the night. Hours of it, taking lumps out of her fragile sleep. A big dog, judging by the deep-throated howls. An angry dog too, straining on its chain or padding about his crate.

He didn't appear to disturb anyone else's sleep. No one else had taken to their windows to see what was happening. All the houses in the estate were dark and the orange street lights illuminated only empty spaces on empty pavements. Even though there was no one to see her, she felt like a nosy oul one, peering through the net curtain in her powder-blue dressing gown.

She retreated back to bed and, wakeful, as she always was, wandered down the same streets in her imagination. She walked through the estate, out into the village and back into the Redlands. She pictured every house, each stingy patch of grass or gravelled front garden. She envisioned the row of backyards opposite, each one as narrow and confined as the one behind her house, high-fenced and always in shadow. Washing lines with room for nothing. No place to keep an animal like that well and happy.

She considered all the houses in the Redlands: the Murphys didn't have a dog; the Strains had cats; the McCrinks had a tiny thing that yapped in the garden all day. She knew Martina McCrink took it in at night and let it sleep with them in the bed. The houses ended with a gabled wall, on which someone had long ago sprayed 'TV licence men will be shot'.

He must be a stray, she thought, wandering the streets himself, considering all the houses for a place to stay, looking for an easy touch. A stray dog – what an old-fashioned idea. There are sanctuaries now and no white dog mess on the pavement. She should probably write to the council.

Her own big bed was cold, for she was only small. Plenty of room to toss and turn in it. Counting dogs was no more effective than counting sheep, it seemed, and they were louder. She had already taken four of the over-the-counter things that evening and they weren't working. She was afraid to try any more.

It took eight weeks to get an appointment with the GP. It was murder getting through on the phone and the waiting room always at capacity. The chairs were full of red-faced people, all staring straight ahead, embarrassed to be on show in front of the neighbours. Marie McGuigan sat opposite her the whole time she was waiting and said nothing.

When the doctor finally saw her, he recommended lavender for her pillow, white noise that she could download somehow, and antibiotics for the chest infection she'd got from walking outside in her nightdress seven nights previously. He was reluctant to prescribe pills for something just on a patient's say-so. People traded medication, he said, and it concerned him. She knew this herself from the odd time Marion threw her something for her anxiety. But she didn't think she looked like the type to do a thing like that.

The surgery was on the edge of the Redlands. From nothing, the estate had bloomed out into a weave of alleys and entries, opening and closing on small bits of ancient green land. There were few shops: the Eurospar, the bookies, Mulvenna's pub. The latter was the only remnant of the old times. In different hands now, it was there long before she was. And long before the little winding streets and walls and back paths. They seemed designed to disorient, but they were put up in a careless rush. A dog might follow his nose through the maze, but she tracked signs: at the gable-end of her street, the TV licence graffiti had been blacked out.

Martina McCrink was out in the garden with the yappy wee thing clutched close to her chest. She was giving out to anyone who would listen and, were it not for the wee cratur, her quivering rage would have opened her dressing gown and jiggled her breasts for everyone to see. Martina wouldn't have cared. She didn't care who saw or who heard. A man from the council had been going round to follow up on an anonymous letter about nuisance dogs. Of course, Martina's thing was licensed and microchipped and everything. The effrontery of it! The council was always interfering, but seemed to do nothing. The McCrink dog chased the man from the gate and he never came back.

So, they never found the dog. Although, after weeks of restless listening, she herself had narrowed down its location, somewhere between the Murphys and the Strains. Maybe there was a gap between the houses and the dog went in there to shelter from the bite of the wind. Or maybe it sneaked into a backyard and all the hemmed-in walls of the tight back alleys bounced his howls around, throwing his voice and focusing it on this one place. The Giant's Ring worked the same way. And maybe the cairn on Slieve Gullion.

She stood at the spot one night, shivering in her dressing gown and her fluffy slippers. She'd bought turkey treats in the Eurospar and had the packet open in her pocket, but the dog wasn't there. The Murphys' garden was a bit overgrown, but not so much that a dog could hide there. The Strains' garden was just a few slabs, some gravel, a Man United ornament. And the houses met perfectly, not a sliver between them, like all the houses up and down the terrace. No space for an animal.

An upstairs light went on as Marion Murphy walked across the landing to the toilet. Marion didn't sleep either; she hadn't for years, not since she'd had her first anyway. She used to say it was the only time she got some peace and quiet, although the kids had left home years ago. When the dog let out a vicious cry from nowhere, Marion didn't even come to the window. She kept her head down as she tramped back to the bedroom.

Some weeks later, another appointment came through for the GP. It was a young locum this time, drafted in on someone's sick day. She thought he would be even less trigger-happy than the resident doctors, but he was quick to prescribe tablets if she consented to counselling as a treatment strategy. He didn't waste time over her history. She was happy to consent to anything.

She would have to go to Newry for that. There was a community counselling project in the village, but the funding had been cut and it was intended for victims and survivors anyway. Either way, there was a four-month waiting list, unless someone stopped going early for some reason. The dog grew more ferocious and his howls more pained than angry. The pills just made her groggy, so she couldn't go out to look for him. If she got up, she stumbled between bed and doorway, then she sat all night at the window looking out, not one thing or the other. The medication blurred her vision, so the dark nights were dark and the orange street lights illuminated nothing. Time moved more slowly when she took them, and a single bark stretched out over hours.

She would sleep in the morning, missing an appointment with the doctor and the first session with the counsellor. They were used to people being flaky, but they had rules you needed to keep. That was part of the process.

The medication muffled her hearing too, but some nights she heard footfall along the street and the voices of men, calling. She didn't see anything though. The animal control men dressed in black were invisible.

They never caught the dog, though he was just as loud as ever. She hated to think of what they would do if did; they sounded just as angry as he was. She never hated the dog. He just gave her no peace. And he clearly had no peace of his own. Eventually he would injure someone.

She began to set the sleeping pills aside. When she'd enough, she would crack them open and sprinkle the powder in with hunks of steak and a bone broth and leave the bowl outside the Murphys' gate. A final meal for him. Put him out of his misery in a gentle way, not hunted down in the night and shot in the back. But how many pills would she need? She never saw the dog. How big was he? How many would be enough? She just kept counting.

The counsellor wanted to go back to the very beginning, to know how it started.

So, she told her: it started with the dog.

And the counsellor asked if she'd always been afraid of dogs. But she'd never been afraid of dogs. She had never been bitten by a dog or chased by a dog. She had never had a traumatic experience with a dog, although she knew of people who had and she understood why they might be frightened.

So the counsellor asked why she was there, if it wasn't because the dog upset her. She said it was the doctor's condition for giving her sleeping pills, so she could sleep through the barking and the whining. She was just a light sleeper was all it was. She had often been woken by men lumbering home from the pub, hollering and fighting. By women crying in the street. By a car backfiring. She was always a bit on edge.

So, the counsellor wanted to go back to the very beginning, to know how it started.

So, she told her: her mammy worked nights in Daisy Hill, as a cleaner. She could never sleep until her mammy got home. Mammy always had to get a lift with someone, sometimes with someone she knew, sometimes with a stranger.

And did anything ever happen to her mother?

No. Her mammy didn't like her to sit by the window waiting, in case someone saw her or thought she was someone, but nothing ever happened.

The counsellor seemed to want more from her, but there was nothing more to give. A pamphlet in the waiting room had explained that 'person-centred counselling' deals with the ways in which individuals perceive themselves consciously, rather than how a counsellor can interpret their unconscious thoughts or ideas. But, when she perceived herself so flatly, the counsellor wanted to dig deeper.

She never went back. She didn't like answering questions. They were used to people being flaky.

At home, a letter arrived from the council, in which her name was spelled wrong in two places. They were processing her complaint about a dangerous dog in the Redlands estate and an investigation would commence as soon as the resources could be allocated. There was no date or timestamp to indicate how long ago the letter had been sent. They seemed to have trouble with communication in the council and she had no confidence in them to find the dog. She had no confidence in anyone to find him.

She would've put up posters, but she didn't have a photo and couldn't formulate a description. Missing: Dog. Last seen... but it had never been seen. Nobody had seen it, when she asked. And nobody wanted to see her when she continued to ask. They crossed the street or stepped back inside their house. The first few times, the water bowl she left in Marion Murphy's garden overnight was returned with an indulgent smile. Then it was not returned. The bowl replenished itself with rainwater.

They must think her a silly oul bitch, obsessing over a phantom dog. But she was older than most of them and she remembered when there were dogs everywhere, all over the estate, in the village, and on the surrounding farms. You'd walk to school and see one lying there that had been hit by a Saracen the night before; black dogs usually, hard to see in the dark. And, then, farmers were always poisoning other farmers' sheepdogs. No one remembered all those dogs.

But the Murphys never had a dog. And the Mahons, who lived there before them … they moved out in … she wanted to say, '85 … they never had a dog. Or they may have had one before she was born or before she was old enough to take notice. Someone must have had a dog. It didn't just come from nowhere.

So, she went back to the very beginning, to how it started.

The library only opened two afternoons a week and many of the shelves had been cleared to make way for computers, but there were books on local history. The village first appeared on an English survey map of 1609. Before that, it was a plain of religious significance, but what religion, what practice, was lost to time – the Irish conducted human sacrifice, not animal. In 1766, the census recorded two rows of houses at a cross-junction. There were twenty-two Protestant householders and eight Catholic. There was no number kept of dogs, although there was a horse track and a cattle pound and animals came to market.

She knew the cross-junction well, as the High Street of the village, with its coffee shops and constituency office. It was about a mile's walk from the Redlands. What became the estate was old farmland belonging to William Jackson. He had lived a long and prosperous life. His children had lived long and prosperous lives, to judge from the short list of men's hands that the property had passed through. There were photos of the house and portraits of various owners standing proudly; men in suits and moustaches, the occasional demure and modest wife beside them. There was no document of dogs. Although men like that keep dogs and love them.

In 1921, an RUC man was killed in the village. More men were killed or disappeared. In the late fifties, the council bought the land from the Jacksons, building three small estates with rows of tiny houses and unnavigable streets. People came in from the country to live there. People like her mammy, who moved to be close to the new school that needed cleaners.

Tracing one map over another showed that the boundary between the Murphys and the Strains had once been open ground; once a hedgerow ran quite close, but not parallel; once there was an outhouse and a person might have walked the boundary line by chance if they went there in the dead of night. The person might have taken a dog for company. Similarly, the maps might show that a lookout tower was once built upon a football pitch and now both were gone. The maps were not exact. They didn't fit snugly on one another and they didn't show everything, only what the map-maker thought of the terrain, the considerations of the cartographer's art – no kennels, no temporary structures. They were all temporary structures.

She took the bus to the big library in Newry, where there were volumes of clippings from the *Cross Examiner*, the

Newry Reporter, and the *Dundalk Democrat.* When she told the pretty young librarian that she was doing research on a dog, she nodded. There were no reported dog deaths, no fitting tributes, no terrible accidents that counted dogs among the lost. Although, in Forkhill, a cavalier King Charles spaniel had chased the secretary of state around the village in front of the press. Perhaps she was wrong to think it started anywhere.

Heading back to the bus station, she stopped into a charity shop to look at the books. The shop was empty and when she called, no one came out. She found a shelf of local history, but there were only the same books as in the village library: a series of local men outlining the events they considered important.

You're interested in local history, a voice said behind her. An old man had crept out from the back room in his own time. 'Yes,' she said, 'I'm from Redlands.' So, you remember what it was like back in our day, he said, and started into a well-rehearsed history that she already knew. As he spoke, she wandered up and down the stacks, down Modern Fiction and Poetry, down Textbooks, Movies, and Music. It was no effort not to listen to him. There was nothing new there. Nothing stuck out, except the repeated name: Redlands.

She stepped into Art, a long shelf of thick volumes and abandoned coffee-table books. There was spine on spine of titles and, almost as the old man said it, her eyes fell on the words 'Red Land'. She pulled out a photographic book: *Red Land–Blue Land.* The front cover showed an upturned gatepost in a field of yellow grass, with clouded hills and hedges in the background. Or maybe it was a concrete battering ram discarded in the landscape.

The old man went on, as she leafed through the glossy pages. He had started and would go through until he had run his course. To him, she was neither there nor not there.

It didn't look like Redlands, the place in the book. There were no buildings and the spaces were overgrown with tall grasses and thorny bushes. Nature run amok. It was only a few pages in that she saw, in the grass, the signs of human intervention: discarded cartridges and casings; the fallen gatepost, a short-term military build, with numbers up the side. As she went further into the book, the overgrowth parted around ruined buildings and opened on to full streets, streets abandoned in the middle of nowhere, under view of misty mountains. It didn't seem like Armagh. However, the first street was a familiar cross-junction with rows of houses down each side. The houses were red-bricked, like she was used to, and each had a stingy garden or gravel path. Page after page followed the street, first down one turn of the familiar cross-junction, then down the other.

The photographs stopped off in pubs and shops. The shops weren't empty, but populated by grotesque figures, wax-skinned mannequins that stood by counter and shelf. In the pubs, they tended bar or sat gripping solid black pints, their mouths wide open in soundless cackle.

She turned the page quickly and opened on to Redlands. On a gable-end wall that looked like a wooden flat propped up, someone had sprayed the words 'TV licence men will be shot'. These were the same houses that she walked past every day, but they were matte and dull. Even in the photo, the wind seemed to blow through them weakly.

There were figures in some of the gardens. Squat, angry figures with their arms raised. In what would be the McCrinks' yard, a gunman crouched behind a dustbin, the end of his wax rifle balanced on the lid. His black balaclava and night camo looked absurd in the soft light of the spring day, but the glass eyes looking out from the holes of his mask were menacing: two dark, square pupils.

And, in the Murphys' garden, there was a dog, frozen in action; the chain that tethered him to the ground was taut like a rod. He was a Doberman with his brown lips curled up over ferocious teeth, mid-snap or mid-snarl. His eyes, as well, were two dark, square pupils.

She slammed the book shut. The shopman at the counter was an automaton, still going without a care for her. She put her money down and left.

On the bumpy country bus back, she read the introduction. An Italian photographer had spent months documenting a British training ground in Senne, Germany. Red Land–Blue Land, a military term meaning a territory divided into foe and friend. Redland. Blueland. The whole village had been recreated hundreds of miles away to orient young soldiers before they ever set boot there. But they didn't seem to have even bothered to populate it with any friends.

Is this what they thought of you? she thought, looking at her dog. His face gave nothing away. He needed to move to tip the expression to either fury or fear, but he never did. Imagine the young men, shouting and tramping through the Red Land, and making their decisions in a split-second, a split-second that never ticked over into the next.

The first soldier she ever saw was trembling. No older than the boys in her class and they were too young for her to consider shifting, he was crouched in the shadows of the back alley, where the orange street lights couldn't reach. She'd got herself lost in the winding entries and was locked out with the patrol, when the rest of the street was snooping through darkened windows. She knew she couldn't speak to him or be seen to speak to him, as pitiable as he was. He didn't say anything anyway. It was his wide, white eyes that betrayed him in the shadow. He was afraid. And that made him more frightening.

But, as she told the counsellor, nothing happened.

She considered calling on Marion to show her that there had been a dog here, but that friendship had passed now. Most of her friendships had passed. Her family gone. She had stayed in the estate and the others had passed on or moved away.

In the photobook, they lingered. The unnamed pub, with no sign above the door, was Mulvenna's. Margaret Mulvenna had painted the sign herself, gold on black, knotted Celtic lettering. But the army craftsman had not thought it appropriate to attach names to things. It fell on her to complete the scene. The man at the bar, throttling a pint of porter, had the red hair of Máirtín McCrink and he wore Máirtín's beaten old thorn-proof, but his face was all twisted and his mouth opened wide in a screech. Máirtín was the kindest man, who loved his wife dearly.

The women all had their breasts exposed. In the pub, in the shops, in the streets. Sculpted on the same wire frames as the men, they pushed empty prams or squeezed the hands of blank-faced children with their garments hanging open. In the butchers, a blonde woman sat at Marilyn Mahon's till, her white coat open around two hard plastic tits and her mouth a red-lined zero like a sex doll. Perhaps they were designed that way by the master craftsman and the model-maker. Or bored squaddies had done it outside the bounds of the formal exercise, just as they had stolen things from washing lines to take back to their barrack bunks.

These people long-gone and misremembered. The most human of them, the dog. She studied the animal again: he had a strong gait; a proud head. It was only the tether that kept him from running for freedom.

She had been avoiding it. But she needed to know how

she had known the dog all this time, how she had heard his desperate calls.

She turned the page. One row of houses reflected another and opposite the Murphys – the Mahons really – was her own house. The door was the same brown from when she was a child. The windows, stained wood not PVC. The same net curtains. One set, in an upper window, was swept to the side. And there she was, looking down on the spot where the dog pulled and strained. Two watchful dark eyes, fixed on the same place for decades. If the dog were conquered or melted or unleashed, she would watch over his absence. But the craftsman, the artist, had not put her there as the child she was. She was an oul woman at the window, unmoving, her powder-blue dressing gown open and nothing underneath. That was what he thought of when he thought of her.

Another letter came from the surgery. She would have to make a new appointment if she wanted a repeat prescription. That would take eight weeks of phone calls again. Then he would cut her off for not keeping up the counselling. Someone had probably spoken to the counsellor already about her session and how there was no real reason for her sleeplessness. Nothing had happened. But the doctor didn't know that she had forty-eight sleeping pills in reserve.

She went to the Eurospar, where she bought a kilogram of steak pieces in a polystyrene tray. The girl at the counter was laughing uproariously with the girl at the till beside her, so she just scanned it through without a look.

The capsules opened easily and she mixed them up with the meat and the broth. She waited until midnight, then scurried out with the simple offering, to the sacrificial plain. There was no light on in the Murphys, no one was watching, but best not to place it in the garden. She left it on the pavement in front of the house. If he had to stretch to reach it, then he might break the chain, if he wanted it badly enough.

The cold came in and she tightened her dressing gown. He was unusually quiet. Perhaps she had spooked him. She thought she would watch from the window and lit a candle there. The street looked dead, as though the air had been sucked out of it, as though long abandoned. The orange street lights flickered out, one by one. There was nothing there any more.

She started to feel groggy. The drag of sleep pushed on her, but she wouldn't leave her seat. She wanted to know for sure what happened. A terrible pain ripped through her stomach and she wanted to lie down, but, as it welled in her stomach again, a howl came from outside.

There he was. The dog on the street. She could see him trembling.

He wasn't pulling or straining, he was shivering. The chain held him back from the bowl and he threw his head around and around until he slipped the collar. He was desperate.

He put his head into the bowl and wolfed it all. She felt

the pain in her own stomach and clambered down the stairs, through the door, on to the street. He howled and howled.

She approached him cautiously. He saw her. His eyes wet and round. His brown lips folding over his teeth. The teeth were white and gave him away in the black street. They were both, for a moment, between fear and fury.

She reached for him, her arm collaring his neck, and they writhed toward the pavement. She put her hand into his mouth, past the pointed teeth, and pushed until he was sick. An orange mess of meat and powder splattered on the pavement.

They were exhausted. She curled her arms around the dog, now lying on its side, and, for the first time, noticed the eight thick nipples on the dog's belly. The two beings held each other tighter and, for how long, they couldn't tell.

As dawn broke, they rose and they both, one leading the other, walked through Red Land, past Mulvenna's which bore no name, past the butchers, through its ancient streets and open ground, along its sinuous ways and alleys. One followed her nose, one tracked signs. When they saw the graffiti on the gable-end wall, they followed the light of the candle left burning in the window.

She let the dog up on to the bed.

The King of Seatown

Emma Devlin

THESE are the things the sea knows: the King's house is far away down the coast, high up on a shelf of rock. He is alone there. Everyone else left when the erosion problem could no longer be ignored. Whole gardens disappeared. Property values sunk. The King's way of thinking hardly recognises these things. He stays, and he sits in his sliver of a garden to watch the waves bite on the rocks below. That, for him, is good value for money. Nothing grows up there apart from skimpy patches of grass, some pernicious weeds. They have names which the man, his son, can never remember.

The door is locked. The lights are off. The King never turns his lights off.

The sea knows these things. These things are important. The sea knows many things about the King and his family. It has been watching.

———————

The boy is five, full of energy. He chirps about the wind, the sky, and the whales. This is the King's grandson.

He is singing about something.

He is asking about something.

He is hanging off the man's hand.

The man's thoughts are elsewhere. The man is the King's son. He is thinking – and the sea can sympathise with this – about the King. The same thought keeps creeping through the man's head.

Some fish make their own light. That's evolution for them in the dark.

King wrote him a letter. Sort of. The man is still trying to make sense of it. The paper was shoved into his letterbox. The man had recognised the writing at once, had gone up and down the road looking for him, but King was already gone. That had been days ago.

Them in the dark.

The boy makes the man say the new words, which he does without thinking: blubber, blowhole, baleen. They've been learning about the whales together. The boy loves the word 'blubber' and says it over and over again. He squeezes its syllables together and stretches them apart, testing the word's strength. He belts the word out and it bounces down the street. Blubber! The man jumps. A dog starts barking. An angry sound from a hidden place.

The King addressed the letter to the boy.

This is for you and not your father. I'm writing this down so you'll know. I want to tell you about the thing I seen. Your father doesn't like this but you must understand. It's Seatown. I haven't seen your father in a long time. I have not seen you since you were a baby. It's better maybe you read this and don't know me.

The boy knows the King through stories. He enjoys hearing about the King. His list of favourite words includes 'Seatown'. The man doesn't recall ever telling the boy about it, but he must have done all the same. The boy makes his own sense out of it.

The boy has a way of seeing the whales everywhere. He points at shapes and shadows that might be them. Bulbous heads appear to him in patches of shadow. He's disappointed that the man can't see them. This should be perfectly obvious, the boy's stance says; they're right there if you look properly. The man says that they're just shadows from buildings, or vehicles, or trees. Still, the boy keeps looking and finds a whale, a shark, a shark's tooth, a blubber, a blowhole, a whale's tooth, a whale's brain, a seagull, a fish, another fish, a baby whale, a mummy whale, another whale.

Seatown. Sea-town. Sea. Town.

'Sure,' the man says. 'Okay, son.'

The whales are a public event. There are people on street corners shaking moneyboxes – Again! Save the Whales! Again! – and other people on other corners with other moneyboxes – Save the Whales! Save Yourselves!

They pass a man who twirls a sign in his hands that says CRISIS WHALE HOAX. He is pacing up and down like a preacher, and his voice lifts above the racket and delivers a series of rants about weaponised weather systems, weaponised oceans, weaponised deep-sea consciousness, weaponised water cycles. There's someone else not far away, and for him it's the end of the world, the shit's hit the fan, it's picnic time, it's bug-out time.

Save the Whales!

Everyone shouts over everyone else, and the man and the boy make their way through the crossfire to get to the beach. People like the man and the boy can do nothing else except go to the whales and spend time with them.

The sea knows these things, and is pleased.

———————

Eight pilot whales, over the course of two days, beached themselves and will not be moved. In the spaces between them, the sea is stippled with sunlight and seafoam. Someone has dug a channel towards the whales and the tide creeps along the seafront, just short of their enormous bodies. Water pools at their edges.

There are people everywhere. The boy clings to the man's hand. Someone is playing music. The bass rumbles in their chests.

There are groups of people all along the whales' bodies. Shh, they're saying, shh. They pour seawater over them. The boy watches them and the man can hear him join in, under his breath. Shh, he says, shh. From this close, the man can make out the crosshatchings of white scars all along the whales' heads and back. They create a vast map of channels and rivers. Every indent is filled with water. The daylight is cold and clear, and the whales' backs gleam.

They see the woman. She's a step back from the largest whale. Her hands are in her pockets and she watches. The man and boy push through the crowd, stamping over seaweed, to get to her.

'They got two of them afloat again,' she says. 'And they just came back.'

'Same as last time,' the man says. 'There's more, but.'

The woman nods. Her hair is ropy with seawater. The bridge of her nose is smeared with sand.

'This is a nightmare,' says the woman.

'Yep,' says the man. He can hardly hear her.

When did the man last see the King? The man can't remember. The man is surprised he isn't here; he hopes he isn't here; he wants to see him; he dreads speaking to him. The sea looks and knows these things. King's hand on his shoulder. King saying goodbye, all will be well, and turning away. Salt spray on the face. Whip of the wind. The man can't remember when that was. Can we talk, he'd wanted to say, can we just talk?

The first time, there were two pilot whales, lying eye to eye in the sun. After a few hours the people pushed them back into the water. There was applause, there was cheering. There had been a crowd then too. But the whales rolled back to land again, and again, and again – it could not have been purposeless – until finally the tide went out too far and they could not be saved. There was no equipment, no cranes, nothing, that could be found to lift them. No time. Too easy to mistake the slight upward tilt of the whales' mouths as smug, stupid smiles, refusing to accept life-saving help, withholding secrets, enjoying the fuss. The rescuers had thrown rocks at the retreating water in frustration. The crowd, uneasy, had dispersed and left them to it. The man suspects that this one will go the same way, until these whales, too, simply die and are taken away as landfill.

The heat at the animals' core will already be unbearable. The weight of their own bodies has been bearing down on their hearts, their lungs, for hours. Everyone knows these things now because of the last time. The last times. They have done this before. There is nothing on the whale, that he can see, that speaks of its pain. Its eyes are on each side of its head, and each one is cool and cloudy, and faraway. The boy kneels at the whale's head, below the eye, and presses wet sand against its side. The sand sticks for a moment and crumbles away, powder. Shh, he says. Shh.

This place will be rubbed away. This house will go. It's been on my mind.

Seatown.

The King made Seatown. People wanted to be part of it. Letters arrived, Dear King of Seatown, and the King was happy. He wrote back and said, Welcome to Seatown, count among your neighbours: stingrays, selkies, dolphins, krakens, squids, leviathans. Here is your passport to all the weirdness of the seas, your stake for fathoms of the Mariana Trench, and Neptune, and the cores of moons and planets, and all the places yet to be found. The house was filled with boxes and boxes of passports, deeds, ID cards, all handmade. And the golden rules. Be free. Look in amazement. Welcome to Seatown. Once you're in, you're in.

'Maybe we should g–' the man starts.

'Do you think the King–?' the woman says at the same time.

'Yes.'

'Yes.'

———

The second time it had happened, the minke whale appeared in the middle of the night and lay on its side for one whole day. Everyone said that when the tide came in it'd be able to turn itself around and swim away itself because, unlike the first time, this one was closer to the water. The tide would come in. Another crowd. Bigger, but not too big. Nobody touched it. Surely, they told each other, the first time was just a mistake, a misadventure. Young whales, maybe. Juveniles of every description get themselves into bother. The tide would come in. And they waited, and they waited. Some of them, while they waited, went to the whale and examined it as if it were already an exhibit in a museum. Searching the marks and scarring on its hide for clues and portents, maybe, for an explanation, for a reason. They were disappointed. The tide, for reasons of its own, didn't come in. The time came for it to come in, and it did not.

The sea did that.

Or, rather, did not.

The sea has its own logic.

Later, people said, of course the tide came in. Of course it did. The whales were just further up the beach than we realised and couldn't be saved. Of course the tide came in, but the whale was already dead. Of course the tide came in, I saw it get under the whale myself, but it wasn't enough. We were wrong to think that would work, that's all; there, that was a mistake. Next time. Don't get frustrated at the sea. Tides don't just stop. The sea doesn't play games.

Thinking on this, the man hears in the voice of the King: *It's Seatown.*

The sea says, in a voice that nobody hears, The tide never came in because I'm looking for the King.

'Do you think he's gone?' the woman says.

The boy has found friends, and they are working together

at deepening the channel of water towards the whale. The man and the woman watch them.

The sea moves in closer. It's interested. It thinks, The whales will flush him out.

The sea knows other things about the King. The King used to sit at the pier with his legs swinging over the water. He looked at his reflection. The sea, in the double of him, looked back.

There is a sigh of relief in the crowd. Perhaps this time.

'I don't know,' the man says.

The sea, disappointed, pulls away.

'He'll come back,' the woman says.

'It's different this time,' the man says.

The boy and his friends have abandoned the channel and have started to push and pinch the mound of sand into strange, elongated shapes.

'I really thought he'd be here,' says the man.

'Me too,' says the woman.

And me, says the sea, though nobody notices.

The music is getting louder. There are fewer people around the whales, more people down at the water. It's a party. People are drinking, shouting, singing. There's a man in a high-vis jacket. He looks lost and embarrassed. Not much to do, not much he can do, not much he's willing to do, with his hands in his pockets, keeping an eye on the eight giant creatures next to him. In case, what? They lie there as the sunlight fades, and their eyes darken. In case something happens. Something might happen, sure. The place feels charged. The music. Bom-bom-bom. The man tries to imagine what it would sound like to the whales without the medium of water between them.

A citizen of Seatown can go wherever there's water, and there's water everywhere. That's all Seatown is. It's not a place. It's just water. You have lakes in your body because your heart and your brain are made of water. Bodies of water are connected. Seatown is the connection. Whatever lurks there might be transformed.

The bass pulses in the man's chest. It makes him breathless. The sea can read the water in him. The man is thinking about every second that the whales are not in the water, that the connection that exists between him and them in Seatown – if the whales can even sense it, if the whales would even care about it – is no use to them.

'He wrote this letter … thing,' the man says. 'To the boy.'

'Oh,' says the woman. 'But you'll have read it first.'

'Of course,' says the man. 'It's that Seatown stuff again.'

The sea knows this about Seatown: The King heard about a decommissioned oil rig in the middle of the North Sea. Someone stuck a flag on it and called it a country. Micronation. The word, when the King said it, split beautifully down the middle. Micro. Nation.

That's pretty poor, the King had said. Divisions. Nothing

would move in such a place. Thinking in the sea, though, becomes oceanic. That's Seatown.

Once you're in Seatown, there is no way out.

But there was this too: one day, before the man was born, the King turned a corner and a car bomb exploded. It knocked him over. It rattled the brain in his head. There was smoke, metal, heat. There was a fire. The King jumped at sudden noises. The doorbell. The phone. A knock at the door.

The King saw, over and over, the same explosion, the same fire. Someone's head split down the back. Lights. Flesh. There was a fire in his head. There was a ringing in his ears. He'd ask, Did you know that, son? Did you know that? And the man, only little then, wouldn't reply.

The sea knows these things about the King: the King found the sound down on the beach soothing. The ringing in his ears wasn't so bad there. The sound of his feet on the path, his heartbeat, his breathing. These joined the sounds of the water: the water when it rushed up the beach, cracked against the rocks, was splashed by dogs, by people swimming; more than the water were the people, whose own footsteps bounced beside his, whose hearts beat beside his, who talked, shouted, laughed together. He was alone, but he wasn't alone. Beyond soothing: it filled him with energy. The sea is pleased with its work. I know you, it said to him. I know you too, said the King. So, the King made Seatown, the sea made the King. These are things the King never explained to the man, his son. The King knows himself through the stories he told about himself. The sea knows itself because of the stories he told about it. And whatever knowledge the man has, he made himself.

The sea asks, So, where is the King?

'What now?' the man shouts above the sound of the crowd.

People elbow their way between the man and women to take photos with the whales. Lights flash in their eyes. The man in the high-vis jacket wrings his hands but, ultimately, does nothing.

The sea watches the man and thinks, I don't know you.

The woman and the man watch the boy play with his new friends. They race around in circles, they stand conspiratorially together, they kick each other. A game with its own rules, which neither the man nor the woman understands.

The woman says, 'It depends. What did he say in his note?'

'Sea monsters.'

The sea says, That is not quite right.

This is what I seen in the water. A mouth drinking and the mouth spit the water out on the coast and flood it. I saw that. And an eye. The water went away and this is what was left behind. Jellyfish and crabs and fish. So much. Too much. I thought I am on an island and it will sink beneath the weight. I seen the mouth go back below the water again. I seen a body moving underwater. Towards me. And I heard a voice. I know how this sounds but I know I heard a voice. I seen her.

The woman nods, looking back out towards the water. Her

mouth is tight, her eyes are narrow. He's not sure she can hear him.

The sea says, I've been looking for him and I can't find him, and I don't know.

She says this to me. She says I've been watching you, King. She says the great lakes of your soul have dried up.

The sea knows this about Seatown: Seatown is the sea, this very sea, and all the other seas, oceans, lakes, and all the water in puddles, pools, sweat, rain. In Seatown, frozen droplets skate in the tails of comets, and among all the dust and the debris of space there are meteors carrying water to planets and moons across the galaxy. The sea is dizzy at the dimensions of itself. And in all of this, the King is nowhere to be found. It can't find him. It can't read him through the water in his body, as it can with the man. There are things in the man, hot and heavy and breakable, that the sea cannot put a name to.

The sea asks, What now? Nobody hears.

'I know he'd been thinking about him,' the woman says, at last. She nods at the boy. The boy is standing apart from the others now, watching them play. She is gazing, no, not at the boy, or the whales either, past the whales, out at the horizon. Perhaps she's looking at the cloudbank, perhaps the long shapes of tankers in the distance. She looks like the boy, who is staring too. 'He wanted to do better, I think. Warn him?'

'Of what?'

'Look, the way he sees it, you're in Seatown too, right?'

The sea says, I have given him whales. I did all this for him, so why isn't he here? There was a fire in the King's head. Things annoyed him. The man, when he was little, liked to run and shout, like the boy himself does now. Until he didn't, because the King shouted and raged about it, for hours. Noise made the King edgy. Noise made him angry. And when doors slammed, and things were broken in the middle of the night, it was because of his nerves. And then: no, I didn't do that, son, I didn't do that, I never.

And the man himself, much later, shouting so much at the woman that she leaves him.

That's Seatown.

I know you don't believe me. I understand that. But you must understand me. Your father is like me. I tried to live too much in Seatown. It was my way of washing out the things I have seen and I thought I could get away. I think I just shut myself up. The same strange thoughts over and over again. I wonder if your father is the same way. I have brought many things into the world. Your father is one of those things. Seatown is another. I have learned. Once you are in Seatown there is no way out.

The sea says, He's not coming, I suppose.

'On the way here,' says the woman, 'one of those guys with the signs asked me about him. King.'

'Right.'

'They did. And they said that if he doesn't turn up soon, you'll have to take over.'

The sign people loved the King. Or they loved Seatown. The Save the Whales! people loved it because Seatown's connective properties tied them all together in a gentle web of life, and the HOAX people loved him because Seatown bound them forever to secret, shadowy knowledge.

'He was joking, if that helps,' the woman adds. 'But you see what I mean.'

The sea says, What do I do now?

The man says, 'I don't know what to do.'

A shape moves in the water beyond the whales. Nobody notices.

Deep in the body of one of the whales, a heart stops. Nobody notices.

The man feels himself sink slightly into the sand. It's not just him. The woman takes a step back, and another. Water rises out of every footprint. The water in the channels around the whales' bodies surges. The boy runs towards them and they take a hand each, and dash back towards the road, up the hill, as far as they can go.

The sea says, Well, I'll take them back then.

The whales roll. Their stupid smiles vanish beneath foam and rushing seawater. All away down the coast, the water rises. The sea says, Once you are in Seatown there is no way out. The drops of rain are implicated in this, the tails of comets, which even now make their way past moons and planets whose cores might teem with something like fish, something like flowers, like birds, and which might crash together at random to create a new thing, bigger than before, a perfect truth unto itself.

The sea says, And I'll take the house.

The sea can't think why it didn't do this before. Water sweeps through the house. Timbers bend, break, and are carried away. The water bursts into every space in the house, searching. The sea sees in the shapes of twisted metal, pieces of mortar, broken stone, the signs and symbols of Seatown, which it cannot read. These things meant something to the King, it knows, and that is all.

The sea says, This is Seatown.

A way off, out in the water away from the house, a heart beats slowly.

Biographical Notes

Jo Baker is the author of seven novels, most recently *The Body Lies*. Her work has been shortlisted for The American Library in Paris Award, The James Tait Black Award and The Walter Scott Prize, and has been Book of the Year in the *Guardian* and *New Statesman*. Her novel *Longbourn* was an international bestseller and is currently in development as a feature film. Her new novel, *The Midnight News*, is due for publication in 2023. She is an Honorary Fellow of Lancaster University, and was a Visiting Fellow at The Seamus Heaney Centre at the Queen's University of Belfast. She is married to the playwright and screenwriter Daragh Carville. They live in Lancaster, England.

Jan Carson is a writer and community arts facilitator based in Belfast, Northern Ireland. She has published a novel, *Malcolm Orange Disappears*, and short story collection, *Children's Children* (both Liberties Press), two micro-fiction collections, *Postcard Stories 1 and 2* (Emma Press), and a short story collection, *The Last Resort* (Doubleday).

Her novel *The Fire Starters* (Doubleday) won the EU Prize for Literature for Ireland 2019, the Kitschies Prize for Speculative Fiction 2020 and was shortlisted for the Dalkey Book Prize 2020. Her third novel, *The Raptures*, will be published in January 2022.

Reggie Chamberlain-King is a writer, musician, and archivist of the unusual. He has published two books with Blackstaff Press, *Weird Belfast* (2014) and *Weird Dublin* (2015), and his fiction and non-fiction have appeared internationally. With composer Martin White, he brought E.T.A. Hoffman's fever dream, *Master Flea*, to the London stage as a musical and his adaptation of J.S. Le Fanu's 'Green Tea' was released through Swan River Press in 2019. He is a regular contributor to BBC Radio Ulster and presents documentaries on the strange for BBC Radio 4.

Aislínn Clarke is an award-winning writer and filmmaker from South Armagh. An Academy of Motion Picture Arts and Sciences Gold Fellowship winner, her debut feature film was released internationally in cinemas and on demand in 2018 following a run at international film festivals. Aislínn lectures in scriptwriting at The Seamus Heaney Centre at Queen's University Belfast, and lives in Whitehead, Northern Ireland.

Emma Devlin is a PhD student in Creative Writing
at Queen's University Belfast, with a research focus on
representations of the nonhuman and envisaging post-
Anthropocene futures. Emma was longlisted for the Galley
Beggar Short Story Prize 20/21, and her work has featured
in the *Irish Times*, *Banshee* and *Channel*, among other
publications. Emma is currently working on a collection of
short stories.

Moyra Donaldson is a poet from County Down. She has
published ten collections of poetry and her latest collection,
Bone House, was launched in 2021 from Doire Press. Her
poetry has received many awards, and in 2019 Moyra
received a Major Artist Award from the Arts Council
of Northern Ireland. Moyra has also published short
stories and essays and has written for theatre. She enjoys
collaborating with visual artists, and worked with Wexford
artist Paddy Lennon on the art and poetry book *Blood
Horses* and, most recently, with artist Jasper McKinney on
a project responding to the pandemic.

Michelle Gallen was born in Northern Ireland in the mid-
1970s and grew up during the Troubles a few miles from
the border between what she was told was the 'Free' State
and the 'United' Kingdom. She studied English literature

at Trinity College Dublin, then survived what doctors now suspect was autoimmune encephalitis in her mid-twenties. Her debut novel, *Big Girl, Small Town*, was shortlisted for the Costa First Novel Award. She now lives in Dublin with her husband and kids.

Carlo Gébler lives outside Enniskillen, County Fermanagh. His most recent publications (all from New Island) are *The Projectionist: The Story of Ernest Gébler*, a biography of his father; *The Wing Orderly's Tales*; *The Innocent of Falkland Road*, a novel set in London in the 1960s; *Aesop's Fables: The Cruelty of the Gods* (a collaboration with the artist Gavin Weston); *Tales We Tell Ourselves*, a selection from the *Decameron*; and *I, Antigone*, a novel. He has been a prison teacher for thirty years and currently teaches in the Oscar Wilde Centre for Irish Writing at Trinity College, Dublin. He is a member of Aosdána.

John Patrick Higgins is a writer, screenwriter, and illustrator. He currently has two feature films in development and made his writer/directorial debut with *Goat Songs* in the summer of 2021. He wrote the online satirical animation *Zoomlanders* for thirteen episodes throughout 2020, and his story, 'Cafes of Desire' features in the first issue of *Exacting Clam* magazine. Higgins' play,

Every Day I Wake Up Hopeful, garnered four-star reviews in the *Guardian* and *The Times*. He lives in Belfast, where he goes for long walks in the rain. He draws for money, and sings in the post-rock band, Blasted Heath.

Ian McDonald is a (mostly) science-fiction writer living in Holywood, County Down. He has written twenty five-novels and many, many stories, which between them have garnered him nominations and wins in all the genre awards. His most recent book is *Luna: Moon Rising*, the last part of the *very* grand guignol and *very* rude Luna trilogy. His next book will be the much-awaited (most of all by Ian) *Hopeland*.

Bernie McGill is the author of two novels, *The Watch House* and *The Butterfly Cabinet*, and of the short story collection *Sleepwalkers*, shortlisted for the prestigious Edge Hill Prize in 2014. Her short fiction has appeared in anthologies: *Her Other Language*, *Belfast Stories*, *The Long Gaze Back*, *The Glass Shore* and *Female Lines*. She works as a lector with the Royal Literary Fund and as a professional mentor with the Irish Writers' Centre. Her new short story collection, *This Train is For*, will be published by No Alibis Press in 2022. www.berniemcgill.com

Gerard McKeown was shortlisted for The Bridport Prize in 2017, and in 2018 he was longlisted for the Irish Book Awards' Short Story of the Year. More of his work can be viewed at www.gerardmckeown.co.uk

Ian Sansom's most recent book is *September 1, 1939: The Biography of a Poem* (Harper Collins, 2020). His second collection of short stories, *December Stories 2,* will be published by No Alibis Press in November 2021.

Sam Thompson grew up in the south of England and now lives in Belfast. He is the author of the novels *Wolfstongue, Jott* and *Communion Town*. His short fiction has appeared in *Best British Short Stories 2019* and on BBC Radio 4. A story collection, *Whirlwind Romance*, will be published by Unsung Stories in 2022. He teaches writing at Queen's University Belfast.